Contents

CHAPTER

I

ISABELLE

I stand before my mirror, tracing my fingers over the faint, white line stretching diagonally across my left cheek. I've had this scar for all seventeen years of my life, yet I still have no idea where it came from.

I don't really mind not knowing. It's a nice mystery I've grown used to. When I was younger, my mom made up stories about how it got there. Some made sense, while others were wildly fantastic. I love being able to pick which one to believe each day.

Once, she said that an angel wanted to keep me in heaven before I was born, and in the struggle, scratched my cheek as she tried to hold onto me. Another time, she said that when I was a baby, I was too perfect, so someone scary and mysterious snuck into our room to even it out with a scar.

She only ever told me that story when I was feeling insecure about something, whatever it was. I think it was supposed to be a gentle reminder that even imperfections could show beauty. Which is kind of a weird story to express that, a scar would even me out because it's *ugly*, but that actually means the scar is beautiful. It's the thought that counts.

My favorite story, though, was the one where she would tell me that my very first steps were taken to save her from a dragon. I fought it and won, but it left me with the scar. I loved that one. I was Isabelle, the dragon slayer. Every time she told that one, she'd tuck me into bed, kiss my forehead, and whisper, "Goodnight, my little dragon slayer".

The sun is almost up, which means it's time to get to work. I tuck a few stray, black hairs back into the braided halo on my head and run my hands over the legs of my scratchy, stiff jumpsuit—the standard uniform for all the servants—to smooth out as many of the wrinkles as I can.

I can usually keep my hair in this style for about a week before it needs to be redone. I don't think I've had my hair out of this braid for more than two days since I was nine.

It gives me the convenience of being bald without having to chop off all the hair my mom used to love running her hands through, styling it in every way she could imagine. She used to just beam anytime people would point out how similar we looked with our matching black hair and blue eyes.

My only two jobs in the palace are tending to parts of the garden and helping to serve meals. Nothing too complicated or hard, just enough to fill my day and keep me moving.

This is the best time of year for the garden job, and I would know since I have it year-round.

The sun warms my skin without burning, and the plants are finally bursting with color after weeks of nothing but tiny green sprouts, pushing their way through the soil.

I'm tending to the blue flowers with specks of purple that smell vaguely like cinnamon and vanilla, Night's Petal, my favorite, when I spot Ryder from across the garden walking with his first teacher of the day.

I think this one is outdoor skills. I can't imagine why he, of all people, would need that kind of training. His whole life is mapped out, and none of it involves much knowledge about plants. Still, here he is, strolling across the garden, listening intently to his teacher, with the elegance and rightful confidence of someone who knows exactly how important they are.

Ryder is the firstborn prince of Adhara, groomed all nineteen years of his life since the moment he could talk to succeed his uncle, Barret, as Adhara's representative in Dominant Point.

Dominant Point was made as a compromise a few hundred years ago when tensions between the kingdoms were reaching their breaking point. People had started to get frustrated that those who dictated their lives were solely in that position because of their birthright.

Tensions were building, war seemed inevitable, but before the first drop of blood could be spilled, the royals proposed a solution. They would form Dominant Point, a council with final authority over every major decision across the kingdoms.

No kingdom could make significant, life-altering choices without Dominant Point's approval. But the catch was that the members would only be royals. One representative from each of the seven kingdoms, Polaris, Adhara, Pollux, Sirius, Altair, Acturus, and Cassiopeia. Each kingdom would select an heir to be trained from birth for their spot in Dominant Point.

That way, the world would still be led by royal blood, but now there would be a group that could fight for *all* kingdoms, and not just their own.

Fair enough. Enough to make everyone a little unhappy, but that's how peace is made.

Ryder's face remains neutral, as if he doesn't even see me. But as he gets closer, he shifts just slightly and discreetly passes me a blackberry pastry behind his back, careful to make sure his teacher isn't looking. Then, without a word or glance in my direction, he walks by.

We try not to make our friendship too obvious, mostly because of his father, but anyone who knows him or notices anything beyond the title of future Achara representative would see that we're friends, not just a servant and prince.

He's been my best friend for as long as I can remember. When we were little, he and I would spend all his free time playing and all his non-free time begging his teachers to let me join. Every day it was the same thing: him begging his teachers, me standing silently behind him.

That all stopped after my mom left, and suddenly I had to be the one to work for me to have a room, free food, and basic living necessities in the palace. But through it all, Ryder being my best friend was the one thing that never changed.

His dad, however, still has no idea of our friendship. As long as it's not about lessons or how Ryder presents himself, the king doesn't seem to notice anything about him.

I couldn't imagine my life without him by my side. Although I could live with it if he hadn't been around for my most embarrassing phases. Like when I was absolutely *convinced* that mermaids were real and they were hidden deep in the ocean, just waiting to be discovered. Ryder never stopped teasing me about it.

I spend hours out in the sun tending to the wide range of plants meant for my care. I'm incredibly grateful to Queen Luana for giving me these two jobs.

I've been around plenty of royalty over the years. By now, I've stopped seeing them the way others do, like gods, so untouchable and perfect they're barely human.

Still, there's an undeniable aura about some of them, probably because it's clear they *do* see themselves as Gods.

But I never felt that way with Luana. To me, she was always just my best friend's mom. She never held her worth above anyone else's, despite the crown on her head.

When Ryder and I would have sleepovers in his room as children, she would tuck me in just the same as she did for him. When my mom was too overworked and exhausted, Queen Luana was the one who would help me fix my hair.

At first, she was only kind to me because she saw how much I meant to her son.

I think she appreciated the fact that Ryder had a real friend, not another person who only saw his title. Then I think she felt sorry for me after my mom left, so she took me under her wing a little bit. She knew that King Henry couldn't know about how close me and Ryder were, so our interactions had to stay limited.

King Henry always paid more attention to his wife than to his kids. She nearly completely ignored me in his presence, but every interaction I've had with her when Henry wasn't around was kind and gentle. She's always felt like a safe place. When my mom was here, she was amazing and I felt no need to replace her space, but Luana was and still is loving in a way that feels uniquely special and motherly. She'll look at you like she cares more about your well being than anything else in the world.

After my mom disappeared, I knew that I would have to start working. I was no longer just one of the servants' kids, I was a servant.

I had watched my mom come back to our room some days with exhaustion so crushing that it was like she hadn't slept in days.

Sometimes she really hadn't.

I was only nine, and the thought of living like that, working from dusk to dawn and drowning in it, terrified me. So when I went to Luana to ask which jobs I needed to take on, I just broke down. I sobbed as hard as my little body could. The weight of everything just broke out: my mom had loved me so little that she left without saying goodbye, I may not have ever had another moment of calm again, and I would be alone for all of it. Queen Luana held me the whole time.

Once my breathing steadied, she gently suggested gardening– she said some people love it–and to help serve meals. She even said I could sneak a few teats here and there, as long as no one saw.

Every day since then, I've been thankful for her every time I go back to my room without feeling the crushing weight of being terribly overworked the way my mom had been.

I did end up finding a love of gardening. Watching each plant move from a seed to a sprout and finally blossom into whatever beautiful thing it was meant to be is soothing.

The bell signaling that it's time for lunch rings in even chimes, echoing through the palace grounds for ten strokes before I'm in the kitchen and the bell has stopped. As soon as I set my eyes on the dishes ready to be brought out, I remember exactly why I like this job too.

I get the first pick of just a few pieces of whatever I can pick off without being noticed. Best two jobs in the whole palace

CHAPTER 2

ISABELLE

I stand still as a mindless statue, just like all the other servants as the Adhara family takes their places at the grand table. King Henry, towering and strong with a presence that commands any room to his attention, sits at the head of the table alongside the regal and composed Queen Luana. At the far end, Crown Prince Liam takes a graceless seat next to Ryder.

The two brothers look like a total mix of both parents, both clearly taking more after one parent than the other.

Ryder has dark brown hair with piercing green eyes, Liam, on the other hand, has brownish–blonde hair with blue eyes, giving him a lighter appearance.

They look like the same statue, only painted with different colors, and just a few unique details for each brother. Ryder got the dimples; Liam is a bit more muscular. They have just enough similarities and differences to perfectly embody the essence of two brothers.

I crack a small smile at Ryder, but he doesn't smile back.

He maintains the collected attitude he has been trained to have. His face remains an unreadable mask of control. But beneath the surface something is visibly wrong. It's subtle, almost impossible to notice unless you know him well.

Ryder's been trained since birth in the art of perfecting his mask. In the public, he constantly looks as if nothing is wrong and at the same time maintains that nothing is great.

Complete coolness in every scenario.

To anyone else it would be impossible to see a difference in him now compared to him an hour ago. But I've known him since before I can remember. Every memory I have has been when he was a part of my life, there's never been a before Ryder.

So while his training may be flawless when dealing with other people, he's an open book to me, or at least a slightly cracked book.

Sometimes when he's stressed or angry or sad I can almost swear his nearly black hair gets even darker and his deep, dark, forest green eyes grow even deeper.

He remains the same no matter what, but it's like an invisible dark cloud settles over him that no one else seems to be able to notice.

I stand there with my hands behind my back and my face blank for the rest of lunch, waiting with all the other servants for when one of the royals needs something.

I wonder if they ever feel weird about it, having people wait in silence, watching for them to want something as if some of us are less human than others. Maybe the servants are less human because we live to serve them, or maybe they're less human because they live a life most people can't even imagine.

Probably not, I don't think it's weird anymore. Although I did when I was a kid and I wasn't allowed to laugh unless I was only around other servants. Like I wasn't allowed to show that I'm also a person around royalty.

Finally, they signal for us to start clearing the dishes. I lean towards Ryder's ear as I lift his plate.

"Are you okay?" I whisper.

He says nothing and just nods very slightly. "I've known you since we could barely talk in actual sentences. I know when you're lying." I lower my voice even more, pretending to brush a few crumbs off the table.

He looks away from his plate and into my eyes. From this close the dread is unmistakably written across his face.

"We can talk tonight. Like we always do. You don't need to worry," he offers.

The gravity of his tone tells me this isn't something he should be sharing in a passing whisper.

"Okay," I nod, then walk away with the rest of the servants.

Ryder's been involved in some of the more serious family discussions for a few years now, and he's always remained sensible about it. He's never let himself show any fear regarding whatever it is that they talk about behind closed doors. I'm not even sure he allows himself to feel it.

They've already had their daily meeting where they discuss anything of importance in the kingdom, or anywhere else in the world. It's always before lunch, and the change in his behavior from this morning to right now makes me less and less eager to know what's bothering him.

***

I spent the rest of the day thinking about what Ryder might tell me tonight. By the time I'm back to being just a statue against the wall, waiting for the royals to be done with their dinner, I can practically feel my curiosity burning a hole through my stomach.

I barely feel present in my own body as I clean up the mess from dinner, every movement is done completely out of habit. My mind's too busy to be aware of what I'm doing. Finally, I finish up with cleaning and make my way out to the gazebo in the garden, where we meet every night. My mind is swarming with *maybe this* or *what if it's that* or *it's probably this*. My thoughts are made up almost entirely of different question words, moving too quickly to take the time to form a full idea.

It could honestly be a million things: poverty: not new, and they don't care very much, riots: they would only care if someone's about to storm the palace with torches and flaming arrows ready to meet the faces of every single royal. There are a million things that could be wrong but nothing that would make Ryder so nervous. Concerned for his people and family, sure, but this was different. He didn't just look concerned, he was afraid.

I gaze up at all the stars and constellations in the sky from my seat on the cold, stone gazebo. It has been our routine for years that me and Ryder meet out here once we are done with our long list of things to do each day, even if it's almost midnight by then. The flowers all around us seem to reflect the moonlight off their petals and the torches around the palace cast a warm, sweet glow.

Vines climb up the sides of the gazebo, each column has its own color wrapped around it. A small sense of pride warms my chest whenever we sit here and I get to see my work pay off. It's really beautiful.

I'm thankful that before I was doing any real work at the palace, Ryder would always insist that I accompany him to all of his lessons. He'd tell his teachers that if I wasn't there then he'd be bored to focus.

There are only a few things that I remember paying attention to, most of the time we were playing and talking instead of actually listening. One of the few things that I do remember is being taught about the stars and the constellations.

Each of the seven kingdoms is named after one of them. Polaris, Sirius, Cassiopeia, Adhara, Pollux, Acturus, and Altair. I think one of his teachers said it was supposed to be a reminder that no matter how important each kingdom might seem, they're all insignificant the moment you look up at the vastness of all the stars in the sky. I'm not entirely sure though, that was another time when we were talking instead of listening.

I try to calm myself with the reminder that if something was terribly wrong, if there was anything to be truly worried about, I would be seeing it throughout the whole palace.

Honestly, I know that whatever Ryder has to tell me can't be that bad. If it were, the palace wouldn't be running as smoothly as it always does. There would be some degree of chaos, something noticeable. There would be tension, chaos, cracks in the smooth routine. So far everything has seemed fine. But seeing Ryder of all people have such a strong feeling of dread so semi–obviously seen on his face, is enough to believe there is about to be a hundred-year war between every kingdom.

If it were Liam, Ryder's younger brother by one year, it wouldn't be so concerning. Liam can be a bit dramatic. Or maybe not dramatic, more like he reacts to the small things like they're the end of the world, while the truly important things seem to just pass by him without a second thought.

If he's been styled in fabric patterns that have no business together? Oh God the horror!

If the palace had all its food stolen and was being denied produce from farmland as the result of a civilian uprising? Ooh maybe we'll be pushed to more creative and delicious food combinations.

Now that I think about it, I wasn't really looking at the faces of any other members of the Adhara family. I couldn't take my eyes off of Ryder. I couldn't process seeing so much fear in his eyes. He hardly ever showed so much emotion unless we were alone.

A twig snaps and my head whips to the side to see Ryder approaching me. No one else is out here this late. No one ever is. In the safety of knowing no one but me is watching him right now, he makes absolutely no effort to hide the drag in his step, the frown tugging on his lips, or the deepening crease between his brows.

"What happened?" I ask. He takes an unusually clumsy seat next to me, dropping his head in his hands before sitting back up and rolling his neck back and forth.

He's quiet for a moment, eyes scanning the grounds as if he's looking for answers as he chews on the inside of his cheek. He stopped freely showing emotion like this by the time he was eight. But every once in a while he lets his guard down and finally looks human when no one else is around to see.

"During today's meeting, we talked about a new sickness that's started showing up." Ryder says in a low voice. I wait for him to say more, but he doesn't.

"Oh."

"We don't know what it is," Ryder continues, his voice tight and anxious. "There's nothing like it, no virus even remotely similar that we can compare it to."

"Where is it? What does it do?" I ask quickly, leaning forward. My heart gradually beats faster against my chest. He shakes his head, like he's trying and failing to explain the severity.

"That's the thing, it's completely new but it seems to have shown up everywhere. People started getting sick oceans apart at the same time. Suppose it had started in one place and then spread to other kingdoms, that would be one thing, but it just appeared everywhere, out of nowhere, all at once." His brows pinch together, likely asking himself how that could be possible or what it means.

"And what does it do? Is it a stomach thing?" I ask, hoping for something familiar that I could understand. He lets out a quick, humorless laugh like that may be the understatement of the year.

"The doctor who told us about it...the way he described it was just horrifying. People would start off groaning and within days they were screaming without a second to stop, clawing their own skin until they would bleed out. Others were nearly paralyzed, they said every movement, every breath felt like razors slicing them open from the inside until they would finally die. He said blood would pour out of them. From their mouth, their nose, their eyes.

"There were others that didn't have these symptoms at all. We just know that it must've been the same sickness presenting itself in another way because all of them experienced their symptoms after being exposed to the other infected. It was some type of hallucination. They would talk to people who weren't there, cry and beg into the empty air, most of them eventually killed themselves."

He stops talking, his head slumped between his shoulders and resting in his hands. I rack my brain for something, anything that could possibly be comforting. I come up blank every time.

Clawing at their own skin until they would bleed out.

Every breath felt like razors.

Blood would pour out of them.

And the thought I can't let go of, *it just appeared everywhere, out of nowhere.*

How can you possibly ease somebody's fear about that? All the word combinations in the world don't seem like they could really do much of anything to lessen the terror of it.

"It's still new, right?" I ask, holding onto any thread of optimism. He nods without lifting his head. "Maybe it doesn't spread very easily. Maybe it's just something that only a few people can get and it'll die out on its own. In a month it could be an old forgotten worry."

"Yeah, maybe." He mumbles in a hopeful, and completely disbelieving tone.

"Dominant Point has the resources to help. You've even said that their technology is way beyond what you have. I'm sure everything will be fine soon enough." I'm not sure of that at all, and based on the shallow nod he gives me, he knows it.

I finally settle on something that won't make him feel better but it might distract him for a minute, or just make me seem entirely self-centered. Either one works.

"I'm going to clean out my moms stuff today," I mumble, feeling a little ridiculous for my sudden change in topic. He looks up from his twisted and folded hands.

"Really?" His brow slightly cocks up.

"Mhm." I nod. I hadn't even considered it in over a year. Every time I bring myself to even look at any of my moms belonging with the thought of finally sorting through them, I just can't bring myself to do it.

Having everything on her side of the room exactly as she left it makes it feel less like she's been gone for eight years. More like maybe she went out to get us something from the bakery and I'm just waiting until she gets home.

I haven't even touched her bedding, other than to smell her pillow every once in a while. Her scent faded years ago but when it was there it was like a lifeline. I would hold her pillow out in front of me, careful not to replace her smell with my own, and lay my head down on the bottom corner of her blanket.

For a moment it felt like I was laying on her chest again before I got too old and embarrassed to sometimes share a bed with my mom. I could smell her hair and the home-made cream she scented with Night's Petal flowers that she always rubbed behind her ears.

It was like she was still next to me. Every once in a while, I'll hold her pillow close, press it tight to my face and see if maybe any of the fibers still remember her, but for the past six years they've given me nothing.

"What made you decide to do it now?" he asks, his voice gentle but curious.

I didn't, I think but don't say, I was just trying to distract you for a second.

"I figured it was time to get it over with." I lie. In truth, I would have been fine letting her things collect a few more years' worth of dust. Ryder nods.

"Do you want some help?" he offers, reaching his hand out for mine.

"No, it's okay, I got it." I shake my head. I think I could just tell him I did it and never actually even look under her bed. Or for tonight let him believe that I'm going to do it then maybe tomorrow tell him I chickened out.

All I need to do is take his mind off of what he told me tonight. Being worried about how your friend is dealing with something is probably less upsetting than the fear that all your people will die suffering horribly. But maybe I really should go ahead and get it over with.

"Okay, If you do end up deciding you want your friend with you, you can come get me. I'll be there, Isa." He squeezes my hand firm yet softly in his. He only ever calls me Isa instead of Isabelle when he's trying to be gentle.

"I know, thank you," I say. Even though I only said it to distract him it's really nice to know he's still here for me, just like always, even when there are much worse things happening.

He smiles, making the unpleasant promise of going through my mom's stuff all worth it, and pulls me forward into a hug. I don't ever like to talk about my mom, but this right now it's worth it.

There's no trace of our previous conversation in his expression or his fear of what may happen. There's only my best friend, squeezing my hand and holding me close when he thinks I need it.

And I let him believe I need it, that I need him to be here for me right now. Because right now that's what he needs.

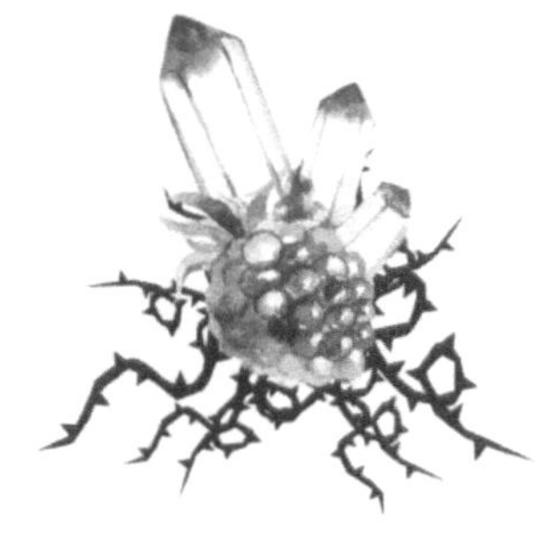

CHAPTER 3

Isabelle

I plant my knees and the palms of my hands on the dusty, hard floor leaning my head down to look under her old bed. This entire side of the room has gone untouched for seven years. I can't see much of what's under the bed, just enough bumpy shadows to show the forgotten things hidden away under there.

The space feels like a forgotten secret, one that teases me with all the belongings of my mother that I would love and hate to see.

I hold the small, flickering flame from my nightstand candle a little further out, but it barely makes a dent in the darkness. I can only imagine how many bugs and mice must've made a home under there by now. It's okay, maybe once all her things have been cleared out I'll push our two beds together to make one massive one. Or one average one, our beds are pretty small.

Yeah, I'll have twice as much bed and maybe some new things, think about that, not the mice and spider families lurking behind the shadows.

I blindly sweep my hand under the bed and after brushing against three more spiders than I would have liked, zero would have been best, I have everything out in front of me, coated in a thick layer of dust.

There isn't much. None of the servants ever have many things to hold onto. It's not that we aren't paid enough, but with us wearing the same uniform everyday and having basics like soap provided for us then there isn't much need to hold onto stuff other than sentimental items.

That's what most of this is: baby photos of me, pictures from birthdays, a lot of pictures of me. I remember her always taking incredibly good care of her camera.

They're widely available but too expensive for most people to own, and the ones we do have access to are grainy, providing nowhere near the kind of quality that royal photos have. She was so careful with it, now it's covered in dust with a strap that looks chewed through by mice. At least she made good use out of it, this really is mostly just pictures of me.

She does have much more clothing than I was expecting though. Enough to make seven decent outfits, more if you're not picky about looking nice.

These clothes are actually pretty, and they're not scratchy at all. I will definitely be keeping these.

The only clothes I have now are my uniform—a black one piece jumpsuit made of stiff fabric that makes a faint, obnoxious rustle whenever it rubs together—two night gowns, and one good outfit for going into town with. A long, plain gray dress with long, flowy sleeves and a deep square neckline. I saved up my money to get this dress when I first started working.

When I bought it it was plain and unworthy of a second glance but the fabric was so, *so* soft. Wearing it feels like being naked under a soft, fuzzy blanket, like the one I took from Ryder a few years ago.

I've covered the bottom of the dress and the ends of the sleeves in a patchwork of blue, pink, purple, red, and yellow floral embroidery. It took forever to be able to buy that much thread in so many different colors.

It's sloppy, and threads stick out here and there and not all of them look like flowers, but it adds some color and beauty. I own that dress and my two pairs of pajamas.

I adore my outfit for going into town but my clothes pale compared to the softness of hers.

Aside from the clothes and photos there's only one item left, a journal. The first entry is dated to about eight months before she left.

I shut the book gently and trace my fingers over the worn leather cover, appreciating the weight of it in my hands. This is my *mother's* journal, a direct window into her thoughts and feelings. I could figure out why she went away, if she plans on coming back, what I did wrong to make her leave, or at the very least I could get to know her again.

She's been gone for so long that my memories of who she was have blurred and faded over the years. But this..this is the real her. Her voice, her feelings, her thoughts. It's her, right here in my hands.

CHAPTER 4

ISABELLE

I've spent the last hour sitting in the same spot on the dusty floor, completely absorbed in her journal. It feels like reuniting with her after years of separation. I loved my mom dearly, and I think, at one point, she loved me too.

Reading her journal is like getting to know her all over again but in a way that feels so raw and real. With every page I turn I get to learn more about the things she thought about most and the feelings she never shared out loud.

I get to know her in such a private, intimate way. So much more than I ever knew her, all without ever seeing her again. Apparently, she's from Polaris and had me there, not in Adhara, like I had always believed.

There are both big and small details about her in here and I soak up every one of them. I've spent the last eight years wondering what happened that made her leave.

She had made me feel so loved, so wanted, what changed? I used to stay up for hours replaying every memory, trying to figure out what I had done wrong to make her stop loving me. Not only to stop loving me but to hate me so much she had to leave me behind.

Maybe it wasn't one specific thing, I thought. Maybe I, as a person, was unlovable in some fundamental way.

But reading this has given me my mom back in at least one way. She did love me. She really loved me. She wrote about how when she gave birth to me and first saw me, she loved me so deeply it hurt.

She wrote about how her heart would swell with love as she watched me sleep. She wrote about moments we shared that I don't even remember how much every single one of them meant to her. She loved me so much in a way I can't even fully comprehend.

I flip to the next page and something catches my attention. It's dated to the night before she left. Her handwriting is rushed and frantic, completely unlike any of the previous entries. I hold my thumb over the page to save my place and flip through the rest of the book. Every page after this entry is blank.

I heard something I wasn't supposed to hear, saw something I wasn't supposed to see, a secret. I know it's something I can't know, can't have seen, and I know that they won't let me have it, that secret.

But it's too late and God help me because it's too late for me to go back and unhear it.

When I went to visit Polaris and see home again, I went to Dominant Point to see a friend of mine. I was looking around for him and heard two people talking through the door. I wouldn't have eavesdropped, I really wouldn't have, but the room looked so strange, I was curious.

It was all white and sleek. It looked so sterile, so out of place with the rest of the world. I know that the higher ups like the royals have technology that we don't have and I thought maybe the room just looked so foreign because they have technology that is foreign to us, maybe that changes the way that they choose to set up their space. But I've worked as a servant for years, I live in the palace and I've seen that they have technology that seems like a dream to most people. Like their devices that allow them to contact Kingdoms all the way on the other side of the globe in seconds, a phone. But none of the rooms in that palace, and I've cleaned all of them, looks so...meticulous, pristine.

I was curious and I only listened for a second until I heard part of the secret. How was I supposed to have walked away so easily after that? It was Barret talking, the Adhara representative. I've seen him a few times at the Adhara palace. He was telling them about what a doctor had told him. He had a patient that had something the doctor had never seen before. He spent days clawing at his own skin, claiming every vein in his body felt excruciating, having conversations with people that weren't there, people that scared the sick man, it took him days to die and when he finally did, it was after a glass like razor pierced his neck. But he wasn't cut by anyone, he didn't even cut himself, the blade came out of his own skin.

That wasn't the secret.

Barret said that he had the doctor deliver the dead man's corpse to him. They extracted countless samples from the body. They got test subjects, unwilling test subjects, and gave the samples to all of them. Every single one of them got sick. They got more unwilling subjects and put them in the same room as the sick for just a few hours, they didn't even touch each other. Every single one of them got sick. And every single one of them died. He didn't just tell them, he showed them.

He hit something, some small button in his hand, and a large, rectangular screen slowly came out of the ceiling, I have no idea how. He hit another button and the screen changed from black to a picture. A moving picture with sounds. It took me a while to recognize that it was a video. I had heard people say that those existed too but since I never saw one in the palace I assumed people were making up stories.

He showed on the video everything that the doctor had described. The second round of forced infected, screaming, running their fingers over their skin like they either need to sooth every part of them self or needed to rip something out, blood streaming from some patients eyes, others begging people who aren't there to leave them alone, others just layed still unable to move an inch without screaming out, the fucking screaming. That god awful, gut wrenching screaming, I can still hear it. Everytime it gets quiet I think I can still hear those God awful, blood curdling screams.

"Day three." He pushes another button

"Day four." Pushes the button

"Day five." Pushes the button

He kept going through each day with the excitement of someone who may be showing a new family pet or newborn child, like he's proud of what he's showing. He goes through days and days until every one of them is dead. Not all of them had even died from the virus itself. The people that were talking, begging for things that weren't there to leave them alone killed themselves. They ripped open the skin of the other dead patient in their room and used one of their crystals to slit their own wrists.

"This shows how far they will go, the fear this virus can really produce." Barret had said with a smile.

That wasn't the secret.

Barret told them how they could weaponize it. He told them that they were able to reproduce the disease itself in a lab using samples from the new corpses, corpses of the people they killed, and they could make hundreds more, thousands more isolated samples of the disease easily. Everyone knows that royals have technology that we will never have, we have been fine without it anyway, but we were told that all higher ups have the same amount. Nothing that the royals would have could do what they can do.

Everyone in the room stared at Barret like he was a monster, by the time he was done talking they looked at him like he was a genius. An angel with the perfect plan to protect them from the comfort of their high seats above everyone else in this world. He said that of course they wouldn't use it now, of course they would never want to hurt their own people. It's their job to protect the people and obviously they would never do anything to hurt them. BUT, they could have it as a production. People get bored and they start looking for problems, often they look for those problems in the government, and that boredom that caused them to look for trouble starts a war. There are billions of people, there are not even a hundred legitimate royals. Barret explained to them that the next time there are whispers, faint whispers of people wanting the government to change, they will lessen the numbers. Once it's all over there will be no memory of a rumor that war may happen, there will only be the grieving of loved ones, the fear left behind that strengthens how thankful people are that Dominant Point helped them, and the abundance of resources now left for the living. No one would want to fight a life with a government that was nothing but supportive during the spread of the illness, found a cure, and then having the resources of billions divided among a couple million, maybe even just thousands of people.

That, that was the secret, that was when I knew I needed to leave, I leaned back to walk away and when I did, the door creaked. Every single person in the room looked at me.

CHAPTER 5

ISABELLE

That wasn't the secret.

That wasn't the secret.

That was the secret.

My mom's last journal entry has consumed my every thought. Every person I look at seems different. I watch all of them with wary skepticism, as if any one of them could be a part of something horrible. Every time I look at Ryder's family, all I can think about is whether or not they know.

Do they know what Dominant Point planned to do? That they're behind what's happening now? Are the people around me a part of it?

I don't think Ryder's family knows. If they did Ryder wouldn't have been so worried about the lack of knowledge they have about the disease.

I can't help but wonder if that was some kind of strategy. What if his parents do know about Dominant Point being behind the sickness and they're keeping it from him? Maybe they want to keep him afraid so no one would suspect they could have played a part in any of this.

If Ryder had known I'm certain he would've told me. He's told me several things only the royals and representatives are supposed to know.

The only one of Ryder's family members that I'm certain about is his uncle, Barret. There wasn't anything after that, just dozens of blank pages. Since that one was dated to the night before she left, maybe that's the reason she had to go.

I've spent the last seven years of my life wondering what I did wrong to make her leave without me, to leave *me*. She had always made me feel so loved, what had I done to change that?

But maybe I didn't do anything. Maybe she left because she was terrified of what would happen to her after hearing something she wasn't supposed to, and maybe in some way she was protecting me by not taking me with her. Knowing that kind of classified information is dangerous, it's amazing she even survived leaving Dominant Point, let alone making it all the way home and having the time to write about it.

Of course she couldn't take me with her, but at least she was able to get away from them. Maybe she's waiting for me to get a little bit older then she'll come back for me and bring me with her once the time is right.

I try my hardest to push the thought of her diary aside and focus on anything else. I know I'm not doing a good job of hiding my panic over what I read, but I can't get that last entry out of my mind. I try to focus on the way it feels to inhale the air, the weight of each step I take on the stone road.

I finished all my gardening for the day and thought now would be a good time to head into town and get myself something from the bakery I like.

Today is just like any other day I've gone to get myself a little treat after finishing my work, I didn't read any secrets I'm not supposed to know.

Nothing's wrong.

I won't have much time over the next few days to go on trips into town for sweets with the Polaris family visiting.

Royal families visit for a few days all the time, but when they do it's always a big deal.

It's supposed to help strengthen the bond between kingdoms if each royal family feels like they truly know each other. It seems to have worked because every time a royal family comes to visit, they act more like old friends reuniting after too long a time apart rather than political allies.

I love coming into town when I have time. The people are warm and friendly, and the town itself has this charm. The buildings are all made of stone with stained glass windows and there are potted and climbing flowers every few feet. It's alive and bursting with color accompanied by bright tiny birds and a few small scurrying critters.

The closer I get to the bakery the stranger everything feels. People seem...off. Everyone looks around like they're on edge. I don't see any friendly acquaintances making small talk or people holding the door open for others with a warm smile. Instead, everyone is eyeing each other with suspicion and keeping their distance from everyone else.

I keep my gaze down as I step into the bakery. The comforting, starchy, sugary, sweet scent of freshly baked bread and pastries immediately fills the air and floods my nose

"One vanilla cupcake please," I say to Ms. Pearl, the bakery owner, with a smile.

She's a large part of the reason why this is my favorite bakery. She reminds me of a grandma.

She has long, all-gray, almost white hair and every one of the many wrinkles on her face gets filled in when she smiles. I like that you can see the evidence of every smile that's ever grazed her face, it makes her look bright. She's like sunshine and hugs wrapped up in the form of a person.

Every time I come in she gives me a warm smile and tells me to have a nice day with some sort of sweet nickname, like hun or sweetheart.

But today, she hands me my cupcake in a paper bag without a single word or a smile. Her lip doesn't even curl up a little past a frown.

"Thank you." I saw, still smiling at her. She gives no goodbye or smile, just watches me closely as I walk out the door. I never thought I would be so eager to get back to the palace and start working again.

Everything feels so tense. It's like reading a long, drawn out build to a scare in a book and I'm not interested in being a part of it.

I start to curve around the back of the bakery and take a shortcut to the palace when, out of the corner of my eye, I catch a glimpse of a frail looking old man with glasses and thinning gray hair coughing.

I don't think much of it other than wondering why coughs sound increasingly disgusting the older we get. He's old, old people cough, it's okay.

I look back over my shoulder at him, and right as I do I watch him fall to the ground as a fresh steak of blood that wasn't there just a second ago trickles down his forehead. A bloody rock sits on the ground next to him. It seems almost impossible that he was just coughing a second ago, and now he's on the ground with blood streaking down his face.

I whip my head side to side, trying to see who threw it as I step closer to help him. How could anyone throw a rock at someone who clearly doesn't feel well? Much less one that barely seems able to stand.

Before I can see who threw it or get a step closer to help him another one goes flying through the air, then another from a different angle. More and more people pick up whatever heavy thing is closest to them, a rock, half a brick, and all of them pull their shirts up to cover the lower parts of their faces.

I hear sickening cracks of bone meeting rock louder than they should ever be heard, grunts and soft, fading pleas coming from the man on the ground.

"Please." He holds out his trembling hand and cries, "Please stop. Please." A sob shakes his body, followed by another. He grunts and cries and pleads for people to stop.

I try to push past a couple of people in the back of the crowd.

"Stop! What are you doing?!" My voice cracks as I yell for the people around me to stop. I might as well be screaming into a pillow. No one seems to hear me, or care to listen. Hot anger and terror rush through my veins, making my skin burn with a feeling of helplessness.

"Stop! He's-" Someone shoves me down to the ground in an attempt to get closer to the man. I haven't seen through the crowd since it first formed. My body is tossed back and forth, slamming into the others before I hit the ground again, hard. I dig my hands into the dirt to push myself up as I stumble back up to my feet.

"You can't..." My voice falters as I push past someone. The man on the ground is no longer the frail figure I saw just a second ago, he's become something completely unrecognizable. His cries and pleads have stopped. The only sound coming from him is the sound of each object meeting his broken flesh.

I squeeze my eyes shut, turn around and try as hard as I can to not throw up. Before my brain can tell my eyes to shut, while I am still looking at the man who looks more like a pile of flesh covered in blood than a man, someone throws the final, heavy rock right at his skull. Right *into* his skull. I hear the bone of his skull shatter, I hear the sound of the rock splattering into his brain. I see a splash of blood, tiny chips of his skull, and bits of his brain fly up. I *feel* small pieces of it on my face.

My brain isn't communicating with my body correctly. Every step feels wrong and unsteady, like my brain has given up on my body. I stumble a bit with each step I take. My ears are ringing, my head feels light, and my face is flushed cold.

I make it five stumbling steps behind the bakery before I fall to my knees. I throw up over and over again until I'm dry heaving over the puddle of my own vomit.

He was just here a few seconds ago. He was coughing, but he was *fine*. How can pieces of him now be covering me when he was just here? Whole and in one, solid piece.

I just barely start to calm down and steady my breathing when I go to wipe off my face and the moment I feel the mixture of blood, brains, and bits of skull on my hand, I start again.

All I can feel is the reminiscent of it on my hands, streaks of it down one side of my face and the other side just as it was when it first happened, with clumps rather than a streak of blood wiped across my face. I cry, dry heave, sob, and dry heave, until I've emptied all my yellow bile from my stomach.

I need this feeling off of me. It's only on my face and the one hand but I feel it *everywhere.* It's covering me, crawling over every inch of my skin, suffocating me.

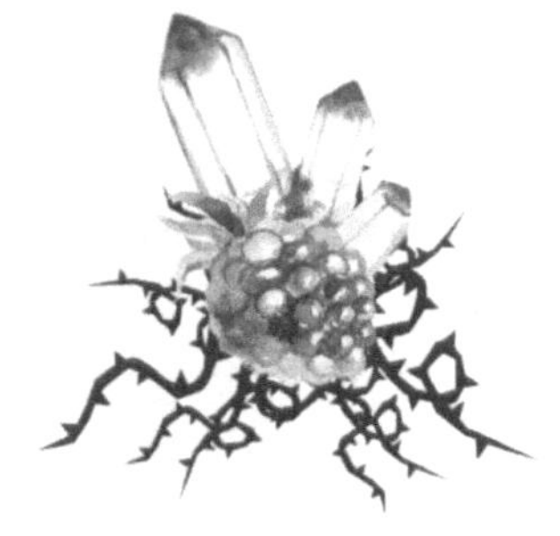

CHAPTER 6

ISABELLE

I scrubbed and scrubbed at my skin in the shower until the only redness left was from my own skin being rubbed raw. I was so desperate to get the feeling off me, to not feel so disgusting with the evidence of something so heartless all over me, that I used my moms old exfoliating stone to scrub my skin.

The rough surface bit into my skin as I worked it over my body. A few spots on my chest and arms even began bleeding. But it didn't matter, I just wanted all of it off, the whole feeling. My skin is raw and burns but I can still feel it on me, little pieces of who he was.

I'm still fighting down the vomit working up in my stomach but I doubt there's anything left to come out.

Oh God, the sight of his blood and the solid pieces of his skull running in the water past my feet and craining down my tub. Going to wash my hair only for my finger to land directly on a hard chip of skull-

My body slams face first into another sturdier and much taller body.

"I'm so sorry, I should've been looking-" I ramble until my words get caught in my throat. My heart and breath freeze altogether when I look up at the face above me- *Barret.* His irritation twists into a smile as his gaze sweeps over my face.

"Oh I remember you. Ivy-wait no, Isabelle. Isabelle Blum. Last time I saw you, you were down one front tooth." A silent laugh shakes his body for a moment until I gather the sense to plaster on a smile and force an awkward laugh of my own.

"*Hahaha.* Yeah it's been a while...anyway, I'm sorry for bumping into you." I hurry past him, my steps quick and nervous, as he smiles at me, looking over his shoulder to say something before walking away.

"No worries, sweetheart." He's visited several times over the past few years of course. But every time, despite Ryder always wanting to be by his side when he's in town, I always end up being too busy to see him.

The first time that I would rather chew off my own hand than be alone with him and that's the first time I've ever been around Barret without Ryder in years.

Ryder.

My heart plummets in my chest. Obviously I've thought about Ryder since I read my mom's journal but I hadn't thought about how close he and his uncle Barret are. Ryder worships that man.

One time when we were very little, before Ryder had been taught to never ever show others this much 'weakness', he cried to me about how badly he wished Barret was his dad after his own father had yelled at him over something or another.

Just the fact that Barret even knows Ryder and I are friends means so much to him. Barret walked into Ryder's room while we were playing as kids. He saw how nervous Ryder was and promised not to tell his dad. He never did, and to Ryder that was Barret showing how much Ryder could trust him.

In Ryder's eyes, Barret had always been the coolest thing since cake for as long as I can remember. I've been going back and forth on whether or not to tell Ryder what I read and this just makes it harder to figure what the right choice is.

He's been training his whole life to join Dominant Point, shouldn't he know exactly what he would be getting into? Yes, obviously the right thing is to tell him. How could I not? But not only would that destroy his image of someone he's looked up to and loved his whole life, it could also put him in danger.

My mother was terrified of what may happen to her because she knew. She was so terrified that she left her only child, a child that she loved, so that we could get away and we would both be safe.

He's the first born Adhara prince and she was just a servant in their eyes. He couldn't possibly be in the same amount of danger that she was in. But as of a month ago, even a week ago, I had seen Dominant Point as the people who are meant to *protect* us. Now, I can't be sure just how much danger Ryder would be in if I told him and anyone found out that he knew.

I go through the rest of my daily tasks half-heartedly until I'm finally sitting on the cold, slightly damp from rain, stone bench of the gazebo and waiting for Ryder. The bench is made of a mix of concrete and pebbles that dig into me uncomfortably. I absently trace my finger back and forth over one of the pebbles as I wait for Ryder.

"Why so bouncy?" His voice snaps me out of my haze. I turn towards him as he sits down next to me. I hadn't realized how much I was bouncing my leg, or that my nail beds had been chewed bloody. His brows pull together in concern as he takes me in, looking up and down.

"What's wrong?" His eyes sweep across my face then down my body as if he may find the answer written across my skin. I start to open my mouth to say I'm fine, but it just feels plain stupid.

I chew my bottom lip until the faint taste of copper fills my mouth while trying to figure out how best to say what's been eating at me all day. I can't think of any delicate or good way to put it besides just saying exactly what happened.

Ryder takes my hand in his and starts tracing tiny, soothing, little circles on the back of it. He's been doing this any time I seem anxious or nervous or sad ever since I was seven and first chewed my nails to the point of bleeding.

It's not just about seeing something awful or feeling guilty that I was right there and couldn't help him. These are Ryder's people and they're killing innocent old men just for coughing. Not just killing him but beating him to death while he begged them to stop.

"An older man coughed when I went into town today and people beat him to death with rocks." Ryder's traces on my hand briefly pause. "I couldn't-" I glance up at his face, only to see him not looking surprised in the slightest. His brows pinch together but he doesn't show the slightest hint that he's at all phased by what I've just said, only concern.

"Are you okay?" Ryder asks, his hand gently tightening around mine.

"What– Are you not–Are you not surprised?"

"No." he says, plain as day.

"*How?*" Horror seeps from my voice.

"People in other kingdoms have been turning to violence out of their fear for the past two days. Adhara's been luckier in that sense but it started picking up yesterday in the Northern side. People have started burning down the homes of the sick while they slept, even homes with children who hadn't yet been infected. It's horrific, but it's not surprising. It's a uniquely terrifying disease. Fear makes people do horrible things that they never would've done before." A grave shadow briefly passes across his face, but he regains his composure so quickly I almost miss it.

"We were expecting the same surge of violence to reach here sooner or later.

"I'm so sorry you saw that, Isabelle. God, it must've been terrifying. How are you doing?" He removes his hand from mine and places it on my back, holding me while I lean my head on his shoulder.

I think about it for a second. I know I'm not doing good, but what really happened to me? Someone else died, and someone else will be mourning him. He was beaten to death with rocks just because he coughed. The people who did it didn't even know if he was actually infected.

I didn't have a scratch on me until I over scrubbed my skin. Nothing really happened to *me*, I was just there. I sigh.

"It feels wrong to talk about how I'm feeling, like I'm the victim when it's someone else who died and someone else who lost a loved one."

"Oh well, how are you doing?" He asks again, brushing over my reluctance to admit that I might be hurt too, even when I'm not the victim.

"I still feel like if I touch my face there's gonna be blood on my fingers." I whisper, my voice cracking so badly the words strain against my throat. My skin is the rawest it's ever been and my hair has been scrubbed more than ever but I've never felt dirtier in my life. It's like I'm being weighed down and suffocated. My body and mind are trapped beneath the filth I feel pressing down all over me.

It's not him or his flesh or his mind that made up who he was being spread all over me that feels so filthy, it's the feeling of watching people I know beat a man to death. The feeling of listening to his cries and sobs while seeing people still looking at him with such disgust and hatred, just for the slight chance he could get them sick. That's the filth that still clings to me.

I want to rip the skin off my body so I can feel clean again, and I'm afraid that if I were to look in the mirror I would still be covered in him. Ryder runs his hands up and down my back then over my hair, tucking my head under his chin.

"I'm so sorry Isabelle. Would you like me to have a warm bath drawn in my bathroom instead of yours? It'll feel better. I can light some candles, and you can use my scented oils. Or I could ask for the masseuse... or ask the kitchen to make something for you?"

I shake my head against his chest. I just wanna stay like this, holding onto my best friend. "Okay. Whatever you want."

He holds me close, running his hand in soothing circles over my back, and the other gently holding my head against his chest.

I wrap both my arms around him and just focus on the rise and fall of his chest with each breath, the warmth of his hand on my back, and his thumb moving in tiny strokes over my braided hair.

CHAPTER 7

ISABELLE

I've been twisting and turning in bed for hours now. I hate closing my eyes. Every time I do, I see that man again, and with him are the people who killed him. The worst part, maybe not the worst but what's buried itself deepest inside my thoughts, is the fact that I recognized so many of those people. They had all seemed perfectly nice in my other interactions with them.

One woman had made a habit of complimenting my hair, saying she still couldn't figure out how to do that style without it turning into a rat's nest. One of the men always held the door for me and gave me a kind smile whenever our paths crossed.

Knowing that the people I had looked forward to seeing in town are the same ones who are capable of doing something so horrible is...emptying? Draining? Terrifying? Disappointing?

I don't know. I can't find the right word and I never want to be able to. I never want to be so familiar with this feeling that I can put a name to it.

It just feels like a hole being carved into me by the knowledge of what someone can do to another person out of fear. Everyone there seems to know each other. Whenever I go into town I hear nearly everyone call each other by their names. It's part of what I loved so much about going there. It has a big sense of community.

The people in that crowd had known him, at last in passing. They had seen him pick up whatever books caught his interest from the library, and watched him order his favorite treats from the bakery. They may have even seen him walking down the street with his grandchild if he had one, and still when they were afraid they killed him, brutally.

Of all the ways to die, that has to be one of the worst. I'm sure that physically there must be more painful ways to die, but this? This is something different. Beyond the physical pain, it must be devastating. It must break something deeper.

Beaten down with rocks in the middle of the street like someone less deserving of compassion than a rabid animal, by the very people who had once been a part of your community. In a moment when you should've been able to go home and rest, and maybe have one of those same people bring you some chicken soup and say they hope you feel better. Or maybe he didn't need chicken soup and he wasn't even sick at all. Maybe he just coughed. Because he's old, and old people cough.

I give up on trying to sleep. Honestly, I don't want to know what kind of dreams I would have right now anyway. Instead, I swing my feet over the side of the bed and head for the one room in the palace that could possibly make me feel any better.

My bare feet press against the cold floor for too long before I finally find my slippers. Each step through the palace echoes as the slippers scruff against the floor. I hug my arms close to my body, covered in goosebumps beneath my sleep dress.

Right as I turn the corner, my body slams against another and they quickly reach out to steady my shoulders.

Maybe I should start walking in the middle of the hall. This seems to be a bit too recurring.

"What are you doing out of bed? Are you okay?" The familiar voice identifies the face hidden behind the shadows.

"Ryder?" I ask, surprised.

"Mh."

"Oh, I was gonna go to your room and ask if we could have a last minute sleepover. I, uh, couldn't sleep."

"Of course." He turns around to guide us back towards his room.

"What were you doing?" I ask, careful to keep my voice hushed. I'm not sure what time it is but I know it's late. One of the best parts about working in the palace is the technology we have access to that others don't.

I can't exactly pick up one of their 'phones' and call someone across the country but I can find a clock in almost every room. I love watching the minutes tick by, tracking every second of the day.

While they're in almost every room of the palace, that does not include the servants quarters and it's too dark to see them now, hence why I have no idea what time it is.

"I was coming to see you. I wanted to make sure you were okay," he whispers. Ryder takes my hand, either in reassurance or to make sure we don't lose each other in the dark.

"Thanks, I'll be fine. It's just...I don't know. I don't know how to put into words how I feel because I know it's a terrible feeling but when compared to the whole situation I can't figure out a way to say it that doesn't sound completely stupid and self centered."

"It's not stupid or self centered to be upset after witnessing something terrible," he replies.

"I know. I do, it's just... needing to go to my best friend or making it seem like I'm the one that needs to be coddled feels that way when I know I didn't get the worst of this."

"I understand. But just so you know you could've been complaining about blood staining your outfit, saying how he should've had the courtesy to die without inconveniencing you and I still would've asked if there's anything I could do to help." My lip curls into the first smile I've had since getting back to the palace. It feels wrong to even smile after watching something like that, after hearing the terror and pain in his voice as he begged his friends and acquaintances to please stop.

The idea of someone watching another person be beaten to death while they sob and beg for mercy and then be laughing and smiling with their friend less than twenty four hours later, feels almost worst. Not only were those people willing to kill him but someone else was able to just move on from something so horrible with so little compassion. It just seems inhumane.

"What about you?" I ask.

"What about me?"

"Well, how are you doing? You're the first born royal son and people are killing each other for coughing in your kingdom. I can't imagine you're sleeping well."

"No, I'm not. But I'm worrying about that from the comfort of a king's worthy bed in a palace full of people bending over backwards to make me happy while my people are sick, dying, and terrified for themselves and their children. I'm not in a position to be talk about how hard this is on me. Like I said, I get it." He squeezes my hand a bit firmer at the end. He always does understand.

He's a prince with a loving mother and horrible father. I'm a servant with a missing mother and a father I've never met.

The way we perceive the world is entirely different in almost every way, and yet he always gets it.

That's part of being friends with someone since you were too little to remember. No matter what, they get you. That's your person.

We stop by the kitchen and pick off a few cookies before heading to Ryder's room and shutting the door behind us.

"Card games or ranting about whatever book you've read most recently. Your pick," he says, taking a seat across from me on his bed.

I haven't been able to stop thinking about his lack of shock when I told him what happened today. His reasoning made sense, but since I read my mom's journal my main 'proof' that he doesn't know about Dominant Point being behind the sickness was how stressed he seemed about it. He wouldn't have been so worried if he were in on it. But even though he still seemed worried, his lack of shock still unnerves me.

"Is something wrong?" He tilts his head a bit.

"No, no, just lost in thought I guess." I realize now that I've been staring at him the way I did when I was trying to figure out if he had eaten the last slice of cake.

He had.

"Liar." He narrows his eyes at me. I chew the inside of my cheek hard enough to bleed before I decide what to say.

"I found something in my moms stuff."

"What is it?"

"I just...It's...it's something important and I'm not sure how to handle it. Do you want to see it?" I ask. His brows knit together as he finds a response to my vague question.

"If it is causing you this much worry then yes I would very much like to see it. But, I won't pry if it's something personal. It's all up to you."

"That's not helpful." I groan. He fights back a smile.

"I'm sincerely sorry but given the little information you've told me I don't know what more to say."

"It's something that I don't think you'll like–I know you won't. But I also think that you need to see it." The humor drains from his face, replaced with something more intense and a little skeptical.

"Okay. I trust your judgment. If you think I need to see it, then show me."

"Are you sure?" I ask, kind of hoping he'll change his mind. Right now I can still hold onto the hope that he had nothing to do with it, that he would never in a million years be a part of something like this. But if I show him this and he isn't fazed at all, if he did take part in this and lied to me about it then he would be just like Barret. Just like the people who made my mom run for her life, and just like the ones who are letting people beat their friends to death in the street because they're so afraid.

He wouldn't just be like them, he would be one of them, and not at all the person I've known and loved more than anything for my whole life.

"I'm sure," he says. If he knew what was going on, he would've probably already guessed what this is about and he would be looking at me much differently than he is now.

"You have to swear not to tell anyone." I point at him, my voice firm.

"I promise, Isabelle, but whatever it is I doubt it could be worse than the worst case scenarios your stalling is causing."

"Okay. Stay here." I get off his bed and march down to my room. With how much I've been chewing my lip since I found that journal I'm surprised I still have one left at all.

Selfishly, I really want to watch him read it just to ease my own concerns. I need to know whether or not he's involved with what Dominant Point is doing. While in my heart I don't think he could ever condone something like this, he's not just the first born prince but also the future Adhara representative. It would make sense for him to know.

Even if he doesn't know anything about this it's still best to show him what I read for his own sake. He'll be a part of this group one day, he deserves to know what he's joining.

But if he doesn't know... my chest tightens just thinking about how this news would hurt him. Not only would it destroy his ideology of what he's been training his whole life to be a part of, but it would also expose the man he looks up to the most as a monster.

Since I mentioned the journal to him I've been more focused on that than on what it would do to him if he actually didn't know. Everything he's lived his life for will have been a lie. One of his favorite people in the world will be exposed as a monster who would abduct innocent people for testing, then unleash a horrific sickness on his own people that would rip through families all for his own gain in power.

I hesitate for a moment once I get back to Ryder's room for a few seconds before walking through the door. Ryder eyes the journal curiously as I sit down on his bed across from him and flip to the last entry.

"It's what I read in here," I explain. He reaches out for it and I reluctantly hand it over.

I watch every slight movement of his face as his eyes follow every word. I know with absolute certainty after a few seconds, or maybe it's been hours, that's more what it feels like, that he didn't know any of this.

My relief is short lived as I watch his expression shift through the realization of what he's reading. Shock, disgust, recognition, betrayal, and finally, anger.

He takes a moment to recollect himself before looking away from the pages and towards me, not directly at me.

"Thank you for showing me this. I understand why you were hesitant," his voice is distant. He won't look at me, or the journal. He just stares down at the blanket.

"Are you okay?" I ask.

"Yes. I'm just processing. That's all." His expression is unreadable.

I nod, "How are you feeling?" I ask.

He shakes his head, still looking down, "I don't want to talk about it," he says, even quieter than before.

We sit in silence for a minute. Part of me wants to shake him until he tells me how he's feeling so maybe I can help. I'm not sure how I would, but at least I could try. But I'll give him tonight before I pry. For tonight he can just process.

"We should go to sleep. It's getting late," he says shallowly, his eyes look far off from what he's saying.

"Okay." I nod and move with him, slipping under the incredibly soft blankets of his bed. I face away from him for a while. It's my ill conceived attempt to give him some semblance of privacy while he thinks.

I roll over and wrap my arms around him. A small noise breaks out of him at the sudden movement.

"Just because you can't tell anyone doesn't mean you don't have anyone to talk to. I love you." I whisper. His breathing steadies, and slowly the tense muscles under my arms relax.

"I love you too." He gently presses his lips to the top of my head. We lie together in silence for a few minutes. This time, I'm the one holding him, rubbing his back, and trying to make sure he feels that I'm here for him just like he's always been here for me.

"What's this?" He asks, tenderly moving the neckline of my sleep dress a little to the side.

"Huh?" I look down and see a spot on my chest that I rubbed raw has become bright red with the beginnings of tiny scabs and a little bit of blood.

"Oh, when I got back I didn't feel clean enough after my first wash." I admit. It looks a lot worse than it is. It really doesn't hurt that bad, it just stings.

Ryder sits up, pulling his legs in front of him and motions for me to do the same. Once I'm sitting up he shifts his focus to the plunging neckline of my white sleep dress, gently tugging it side to side. He finds two more spots like that, silently winces at the sight of them, then softly takes my hand to lift up my sleeves.

"You meant to do this?" He asks. His voice is calm, but there's an unmistakable concern in his eyes as he examines the raw, scratched skin.

I lower my voice barely above a whisper, "No, I just wanted to feel clean." The words ache in my throat as I force them out.

His finger hovers over one of the more severe spots on my arm.

"How are you doing, Isa?" Ryder frowns as he holds my arm tenderly, stroking his finger up and down the unharmed areas. My throat tightens up in an all too familiar feeling while I try to stop my chin from wobbling.

"I couldn't help him." My voice cracks, and with it every ounce of my composure shatters. My shoulders shake, my face pinches together, while sobs and tears flow out of me.

"Isa," Ryder pulls me into a tight hug, his hand cradling the back of my head, while the other rubs soothing circles along my back. "That wasn't your fault. There was nothing you could've done to protect him against a whole crowd of angry and scared people."

I scootch a little bit closer to him and wrap my arms around his torso while he holds me.

"Did you do that to yourself on purpose because you felt guilty?" His voice is gentle yet insistent, demanding the truth. I sniffle and wipe my face.

"No, I swear." My throat is sore and shaky from all the tears as I force the words out. I honestly wasn't trying to hurt myself. It didn't even hurt in the moment. I just felt relieved that it was off of me. Hurting myself wasn't on my mind at all, just being clean.

I'm not sure how exactly to explain that feeling, the words don't even make sense to me but the meaning does. I don't try to explain and he doesn't ask.

"Okay." He runs his hand over my head one last time then kicks the blanket off to get out of bed. He rounds the corner and disappears into his bathroom. I hear the sound of cabinets opening and closing and the faint clicks of jars being pushed around echoing throughout the large, pristine, gold covered room.

I love it when I'm not feeling well and he lets me take a bath in there. If there's a beautiful afterlife waiting for us, it has that bathroom in it. There's something magical about that room, the gold accents, the way the lights spill across the marble floor, it's a bathroom that a fairy princess from a fantasy book would take a bath in.

He rounds the corner out of the bathroom with a little wooden jar in hand. He unscrews the top as he crawls back onto his bed in front of me.

"This may sting just a little bit," he warns while rubbing his fingers over the whipped ointment. It was a servant's recipe made mostly of rice jelly, honey, and flowers. It's used for soothing and speeding up healing.

Servants always have at least a few tiny cuts on their hands. I get plenty from gardening, and that stuff is like a god sent. It even helps with my sun burns in the sunnier months of gardening.

Just a couple of years ago, Liam had some used on a few scrapes after a horse threw him off. Since then the royals have come to love the remedy too. The women who'd made it even got an upgraded room for giving them the recipe.

Ryder takes my hand and carefully pulls my sleeve up then rolls it to stay in place. "How are you feeling? With what I showed you." I ask, then jerk back a little at the feeling of his fingers rubbing the ointment on one of the more tender spots on my arm.

"Did that hurt?" He looks back up at me and away from my arm.

I shake my head, "It's okay."

We're quiet for a minute and I just watch him apply the cream to various spots on my arms. It doesn't sting much. His windows are slightly open letting in fresh night air. I can hear the distant chorus of crickets and frogs, their songs weaving together in a soft harmonious melody. It would be a really nice night.

"Ryder?"

He finishes applying the cream to my second arm, then shifts his focus as he tenderly moves the neckline of my dress to the side, tending to another spot.

"The people I was so excited to join are the same ones murdering the people I thought I would protect," his voice barely above a whisper yet heavy with the weight of his words. He pushes my hair over my neck to keep it out of the way, then scoops up a little more cream. The tender care in his actions is a quiet contrast to the turmoil in his voice.

"I'll never be a part of what they're doing. I've worried that I may not be the best leader or that I may not rule with enough compassion for my people, simply because I'll never truly understand them. But I won't ever be responsible for whole families dying in pain, terrified, watching each other die while other people kill just because they're afraid."

His words hang in the air between us, raw and vulnerable, and for a moment, the world outside seems just beyond reach, waiting to grab us back. For now it's just us here, in this quiet space, as he lays bare the kind of leader he refuses to become.

"But I've spent my entire life training for this one thing. What could I possibly say about why I suddenly refuse? If I don't go they'll know something has changed, and if I do go and I try to change what they do then they'll kill me for being a liability, for not being one-hundred percent with them."

The panic builds in his voice, his words tumbling out faster, each one more desperate than the last. "I can't do anything to help the people even though I'm the first born prince, and I'm not even sure I can save myself." He finishes, the air between us feels thick, charged with the anger and fear freshly brewing inside of him.

I don't know how to make sense of the impossible choice he's facing. But I know one thing for sure: I'll be here, however this unfolds.

"If you can't help your people, that's not your fault. That's the fault of the ones murdering them and letting the royals still think they were somehow in charge. And we won't let them hurt you. If we have to live alone on a tiny boat in the middle of the ocean for them to not be able to hurt you I'll go with you." The words come from deep inside of me, a promise I don't have to think twice about making. He looks at me again, his expression is a mixture of exhaustion and pain.

"He's my uncle. I love him. I used to wish so badly that he was my dad because I loved and trusted him so much... and he's a monster." He accidentally presses down a bit too hard on the last raw spot and I wince, the sharp sting breaking through the moment.

"Sorry."

"It's okay." I take the container from his hands and screw the top back on before placing it on the nightstand. He lays down beside me, and I pull the blanket up over both of us, tucking it around our bodies like a shield from everything outside of this space.

He pulls me close and I adjust so I'm holding him instead. I want him to feel every ounce of care he's always made me feel. Throughout anything, I've never felt alone. I've felt close to it, I've wondered what was wrong enough with me to make my own mother leave, but I've always known he would be here for me. Always.

He squeezes me a bit tighter, burying his face into the crook of my neck. I don't know what will happen, but I know I won't let anything happen to him and he won't ever let anything happen to me.

We fall asleep intertwined just like we have so many times since we were little.

CHAPTER 8

ISABELLE

Lunch is extra special today. The best foods have been doubled in quantity, and the most beautiful dishes are even more exquisite. Everything has been done up for the Polaris family to visit. As I stand among every other servant waiting in the grand dining hall, I can feel the heightened atmosphere. Everything from the polished silverware to the perfect arrangement of flowers bursting with color on the table has been taken to a whole new level of perfection.

The Polaris Family is supposed to be here for the next two weeks. The excitement and nerves of their visit usually die down across the palace after the first day or so. There's some level of professionalism between the royals for their visits but for the most part they hang out like old friends catching up after too long away.

The Adhara family enters the dining hall first, quickly followed by the Polaris family. The Polaris family doesn't have any more power than the other royal families nor do they possess any traits that would make them better than the others. But they are still seen as the sort of top royals, a subtle hierarchy that no one really questions.

That's really just because Dominant Point is located in Polaris. Even though that connection doesn't give the Polaris family any direct power or political gain, the association is enough to set them apart.

After Ryder steps through the doors he's followed closely by Queen Victoria, King Archer, Princess Marcella, and Prince Dustin. Marcella is a near perfect copy of her mother, though with fewer years behind her. They share the same waist length braids, straight noses, full lips, dark skin, and purely confident, self assured presence about them.

The only difference between the two, aside from their age, is Marcella's striking green eyes and Victoria's golden brown eyes. Dustin, on the other hand, is a fair mix between his very beautiful, obviously regal mother and his father. King Archer's the source of the two children's green eyes and Dustin's slightly paler skin than his mother and sister. The two siblings are twins, but nowhere near identical.

Liam was actually supposed to marry Marcella one day, back when she was set to become queen. But then she switched roles with her brother and is now set for Dominant Point. Liam was pretty bummed about it, Marcella is beautiful and funny in a way that I don't really get. I actually don't understand most of the royal's sense of humor.

The King and Queen's appearances are as different as night and day. From his pale skin, green eyes, and blond hair next to her dark skin, black hair with gold cuffs around each braid, and bright honey brown eyes, but it's not their physical differences that set a contrast between the two, it's the way they carry themselves.

I've met, or at least encountered, all of them except for King Archer. From what I've heard, he's a cinnamon roll of a person. He wasn't born a royal, he married into the title through Victoria. And while nine times out of ten when that happens it was driven by the desire for power or glory of being a royal, King Archer has also been labeled as

"Love Struck", "King Heart Eyes", and been said to follow his wife like a puppy.

Victoria, as well as Marcella, carry the unique presence and confidence that only someone born to be a queen could have, or in Marclla's case, one of the seven most powerful people in the world. Victoria's sure of herself, yet modest. She's kind and empathetic to the hardships of her people yet rules with a firm hand.

Her power doesn't just come from the crown on her head, but from how plainly written all those things are in just the set of her shoulders and the look of her face. She knows who she is, and she's clearly instilled the same mentality in her daughter. Those two are true royals. Not people who only cling to their royalty for privilege and safety, or someone entirely unsure if they are doing the right job.

I've never spoken to either of them but I've always admired their self certainty from a distance whenever they visit. I'm a little bit older than Marcella and it's strange to me that someone my own age can have such a fundamentally different life, a different mind. Even if it's not until I'm eighty years old, I want to one day be as sure of myself as she is, to walk through life with the same quiet confidence, knowing exactly who I am.

My eyes stay on King Archer the longest. As the 'new comer' I've never had the chance to meet him before. He doesn't always attend these types of things. Even though no politics are meant to be discussed, these stays with other families do have some political gain in building a relationship with each other, and King Archer isn't one for politics.

He scans the room and after a few seconds his eyes land on me. The moment his gaze settles in my direction his lips part as the color drains from his face. My skin pricks with heat under his unmoving stare and I realize he isn't just looking at me. He's looking at the scar on my cheek.

Someone moves a chair back, making a terrible screeching sound that snaps his attention back to the room around him. I try to meet Ryder's eyes for any indication that he may have seen that but he's in a conversation, or more accurately, an eye roll contest on Liam's side.

I try not to look at the King for the rest of the meal but whenever I do, I catch him watching me. Sometimes in a look of confusion, sometimes anger, and other times it's something far different from the other two that I can't quite seem to place. The feeling of uneasiness doesn't leave me at all during dinner.

I understand that when someone first meets me, it's natural for their eyes to linger on the faint white line stretching across my cheek for a moment, but this isn't just run of the mill curiosity about what may have happened. There's something deeper in his expression, something unsettling, and whatever it is it makes my skin crawl.

By the time dinner is finally, *finally,* over I move through each step to clear the table with an extra boost of speed to my step. I don't think I really breathed since King Archer first looked at me until I was out of the dinning room for good.

I speed walk to my room, eager to get ready for bed, then sneak into Ryder's room when most of the palace is asleep to tell him about how King Archer was watching me during lunch. But I stop in my tracks at the sound of the only voice that could unnerve me more than King Archer right now.

Barret.

He's around the corner I was just about to cross, his voice low and hurried as he whisper–shouts at someone.

"They need to be-" My nail scraps against the wall in my attempt to steady myself, making a noise faintly loud enough to stop him. He turns the corner just before I can get my feet moving under me.

"It's rude to eavesdrop, you know." His voice is smooth, but there's an edge in his tone that sends a cold shiver down my spine.

"Sorry–I'm sorry." I stutter, my pulse races through my veins, every instinct screaming to flee, but my feet stay rooted in place.

"*Go.*" The cold shiver quickly turns to lightning under my feet, carrying me out of the room. I know I'm not the smartest person. I know I've grown up with the mandatory education for servant's children which is far from great. But I have honestly never felt stupider than I do right now.

How could I possibly be so careless? Who in the right mind would read about what happened in my mom's journal and then *still* eavesdrop on a conversation with Barret?! Listening to Barret's conversations when you aren't supposed to be is the reason my mom had to leave and yet I still did the exact same thing.

I can't blame her for listening. A little part of me had been mad at her for putting herself in that position. A conversation with the highest government officials in the *world,* one that seems a bit shady from the beginning? *Leave!* But, curiosity is a very strong deterrent from rational thought.

Everyday since I read that journal I grow more and more uneasy. As I move through the rest of my tasks for the day, I can't help but feel like I'm just waiting for the next bad thing to happen. The King could have some absurd reason for watching me like that during lunch, another person could be unjustly killed while I watch and fail to do anything to help. Barret could decide he's moving in at the Adhara palace for a long time stay.

I'm not exactly sure what I'm waiting for but the anticipation of it sits in my stomach all day.

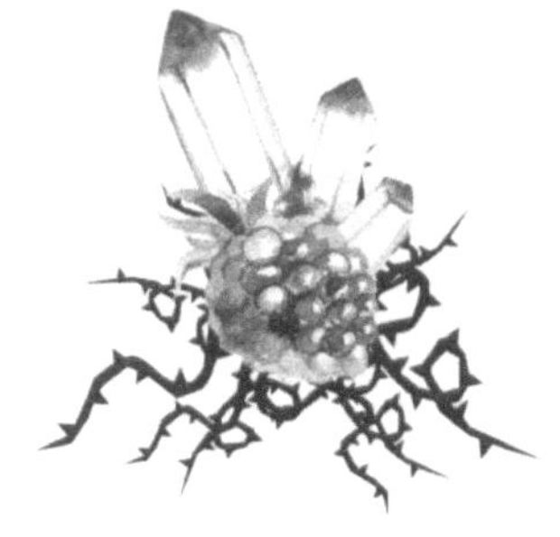

CHAPTER 9

Isabelle

I trace my hand against the wall to guide me down the dark halls. After all these years of sneaking into Ryder's room once the rest of the palace is asleep, I could probably do it with my hands behind my back and a blindfold, even though I might as well be wearing one anyway with how dark it is.

Still, I would rather not risk falling down one of the thousand flights of stairs with a million steps.

I understand why people don't want the nineteen year old prince to have a seventeen year old girl spending the night in his room, especially when that seventeen year old is a servant and not one of the princesses or rich daughters they surround him with. But couldn't they make an exception for someone who's been his best friend for almost their whole life?

I would love to make this walk with my candle stick lighting my way. The flicker of light would've offered some sense of control, without it I'm left with every muscle tight and bracing to trip over something I can't see.

I would take the old servants tunnels, but I've been terrified of them since I was a kid. I heard the sound of a rat screeching and decided they must be haunted, that's the real reason they're closed. I haven't gone back in since.

Just like always, his door is unlocked. He's supposed to keep it locked during the night, and he does at first, but this has become a typical routine of ours and knocking would be too loud. He locks his door at the beginning of the night but it's always unlocked within the hour.

I slowly creak his door open just as he walks out of his closet, in his obscenely comfortable pajamas. His loose shirt opens almost all the way to his shoulders, draping over him like a blanket.

"Ryder, I love you, but if there's ever a worker uprising, I *will* help them assassinate you so I can take your pajamas."

"And to think that I've let you borrow them every time you've slept over. I see how much our friendship means to you. You wounded me, deep in my heart Isabelle." He pulls a dramatic, sorrowful face, before his lips twitch and break into a full, dimpled smile.

"Well, maybe you've just given me a taste of what I want all to myself," I shrug as I make my way over to his closet. One of the perks of being best friends with the prince is that he's always been incredibly generous about sharing his luxuries with me. His ridiculously comfortable clothes are just one of the many things I've come to appreciate.

I emerge back out from his abundantly large closet draped in pajamas way too big for me but too comfortable for me to care. It feels like a cloud brushing against my skin. I hold up the waistband of his white pajama pants, the shirt loosely draping over one of my shoulders, while I make my way over to his bed.

He motions towards the window, and a smile spreads across my face.

"We haven't gone up there in forever," I can hear the nostalgia in my voice. Between his bed, clothes, the amazing water pressure in his shower, and all the other things he shares with me, my absolute favorite is the view that no one else knows about.

"It hasn't even been two weeks."

"Close enough." I wave a dismissive hand. He laughs a short laugh before pushing one of the windows open, and taking the first step onto the small walkway. When I say small, I mean it. There's a reason no one else knows about this view, no one else would think to do something this reckless without the promise of something nice at the end.

He reaches out for my hand, and with a gentle tug, pulls me onto the narrow ledge with only enough room to hold us with our back pressed to the wall. If we fell, there are at least a few different slanted roofs to catch our fall. Still, it wouldn't be fun.

We side step carefully, moving inch by inch until we reach the two roofs connected at a diagonal angle. With practiced movements, we push our opposite hands and opposite feet, against the two walls until we're at the top of one of the intersections of roofs. We maneuver all the way throughout our memorized path until we reach the top.

It's a flat surface at the other side of the palace, a quiet little corner that feels like our own secret escape. The only things here are the two chairs we lugged up about three years ago, much to his reluctance and my persistence.

There *is* another way up here besides climbing out of a window, a less stupid way. A ladder leading all the way to the rooftop from the ground. It's tucked out of sight on the far side of the palace, lightly buried under growing vines, and the few people who do stumble upon it don't think to use it.

"I don't think I'll ever get tired of coming out here," I whisper, my voice barely audible as I gaze up into the clear sky of stars.

From here, you can feel as though you're almost an arm's reach from touching the stars. When you look out you can see the moonlight casting a silver glow on the garden, the trees that stretch out for long enough to make anything beyond them impossible to see from the ground, and the river between them, our second favorite place to go.

The ripples of the water glow at night and the petals of the flowers beside it glow just as beautiful, in the color of their own petals.

We have a few of those flowers at the palace, but unless they are growing right next to the water from the river, they don't glow. They thrive as healthy plants but they don't glow.

"Me neither," Ryder whispers and I'm so lost in the sight in front of me that I almost don't hear him.

"You've traveled all across the world, seen every king-dom and all the most beautiful places the world has to offer. There are tons of places you'll never get tired of seeing."

"This one's my favorite."

I turn my head to look at him, surprised. "How?"

I haven't seen all the things he has but I know they're the type of sights that make people believe beauty itself is proof of a higher power.

"This one is uniquely reserved for my best friend and I. It's a beautiful sight to see but it also holds sentimental value. None of the places I've traveled to hold a candle to that."

"So I'm not missing out on anything by not ever seeing those other places?" I say it like a joke, but it doesn't en-tirely feel like one.

"Not at all. Places are just places unless they have mean-ing to you. This one has meaning." He says it with the kind of wisdom someone his age could only have after getting to see all those places he doesn't care much for.

I don't say anything, I just smile. I like the thought that after all the wonders he's seen, this one being his favorite is because of me.

I love Ryder, I really do, but sometimes it's hard not to think about the difference between us. It's his favorite because out of all the wonderful places he's seen, this is the one with sentimental value. It's my favorite because this is the one thing I have that nobody else but Rycer and I share and I know I won't have many more amazing things that are uniquely reserved for me and my best friend.

I don't like to think about him being a prince, not only a prince but the future Adhara representative, and me being a servant. Most of the time, I don't. Most of the time, he's just Ryder and I'm just Isabelle, two best friends for as long as I can remember.

But there are moments when I can't only see us as Isabelle and Ryder. He'll live the rest of his life seeing all the things I never will, having all the amazing things that mean so little to him. His life will mean something and he'll have a purpose. He'll get to have many new loves throughout his life, he already had one with Anastasia, and I'll likely not ever fall in love. Not only that, but he'll be living his purpose with so many incredible luxurious things just being thrown at him.

When I *do* think like this, it's not just that I'm jealous of him, it's that I reflect on my own self.

I will most likely never step foot out of Adhara. I'll live the rest of my life as a servant with the only nice things I own being borrowed by someone else. When I die, I'll be forgotten as just another servant who was easily replaced, who meant nothing. One day, I won't even be able to borrow nice things from my best friend.

And worse than that, one day I won't have a best friend to talk to and laugh with every day. He'll go on with his life, and I'll be left behind, a forgotten nothing. He'll look back and remember the day's he was once friends with a servant.

It's not about jealousy. I want him to have those amazing things. I really do. It's that I have absolutely nothing ahead of me besides the next day of being a forgotten face serving the food. I'm not worried about being forgotten because I'm not a name in history, I'm worried about being forgotten because I don't think I'll ever matter enough to someone for my life and death to mean something.

I don't often imagine a better future for myself, I know what my life will hold and I don't want to hurt myself by allowing myself to think of all the other things that would make me happy. If I don't dwell on what I want, I think I can be perfectly happy each day.

But when I do let myself imagine, I picture staying with Ryder, maybe even having other friends who love me and who I love even more. I could wear pretty clothes, I could feel pretty, eat good food that was actually meant for me, instead of scraps from the royals and food made for servants, Ryder would stay and miss me when I die, a couple of people would be sad when I die.

In reality, I don't think my death will really matter much. Ryder will have been gone for years by then, and probably won't even hear about it until years after when he visits Adhara again. Maybe no one will even think to tell him because no one will think it matters. Or he won't even ask about me.

But when I let myself dream, he stays with me, and a few other friends stick around too. And then after I'm gone he'll notice my absence, feel it, and my other friends will miss me too. I'd die knowing I loved people and they cared for me as well.

I know he loves me now, I just also know I'll be a distant memory in a couple of years, but he won't ever be just an old memory to me. He'll always be my best friend, I won't.

"Are you okay? You've seemed off tonight." Ryder's voice pulls me out of my internal pity party.

"I'm okay. Just...a couple of weird things happened today. When King Archer came to lunch he kept staring at my scar. Not in the way most people do, where they're just wondering how I got a small scar across my cheek. I'm not sure how exactly to describe it but it made me uncomfortable." I twist my thumbs, trying and failing to figure out exactly how to describe it. He looked...scared, maybe?

Ryder nods slowly, his expression shifting into something thoughtful.

"I did see him look at you a few times throughout lunch. What was the other thing?"

I take a deep breath. "I overheard Barret talking to someone in the hallway. I didn't hear what he said but he sounded upset. He saw me and he got mad and told me to leave."

Ryder's face immediately hardens, a stern expression taking over.

"If you ever hear him talking to someone or you're around him at all when you're alone, *leave.* I mean it. We know he's dangerous. Don't spend a single second longer than you have to around him, okay?" Ryder's eyes are wide, urgency creeping into his voice.

"I know, okay? I won't." I know he's dangerous. It's *my* mom that I haven't seen in eight years because of him. We're quiet for a few minutes until Ryder breaks the silence.

"Do you remember when we first started sneaking out together? We were ten and twelve and you would always insist that we go to the river," he asks. Obviously I remember.

"It's a really cool river. How many other ones have you seen that *glow* at night? And it has flowers that glow too!" I say, defending all the times I dragged him out there. He laughs.

"None," he admits, smiling at the memory.

"Exactly." Some beaches are like that but it's rare. Obviously, when the only known river that glows in the world is right in your backyard, you're gonna want to see it.

A few hundred years ago, people used to think the river was magic. Women who couldn't get pregnant would drink from it, old people, young people who never wanted to be old. Turns out it just has a weird type of algae.

CHAPTER 10

ISABELLE

Over the past week, things have in some ways calmed down and in other ways gotten so much worse. King Archer hasn't been staring me down during meals, he instead chooses to avoid looking at me entirely. I haven't stumbled into any more heated conversations with Barret and he seems to be back to his old self–the guy pretending not to be a twisted sociopath.

The sickness is getting worse though. It's still spreading and the healthy are growing more afraid and violent. The worst part is knowing that nothing will be done to help until Dominant Point is satisfied with the population reduction. Until then innocent people will continue to die.

Children, mothers, fathers, wives, and loving husbands will die and lose each other, all because of people who they will die believing only ever protected them. All that we get until then is more statements saying 'We're doing our best. Rest assured we are doing absolutely everything we can to help".

Rest assured while you watch your children get ripped apart from the inside out only to die the same death because we want to feel extra safe in the knowledge we will not be challenged and we are entirely safe in every way.

One thing that's been on my mind is that they weren't going to use it unless people started to revolt. Nothing happened that should've triggered Dominant Point to unleash the sickness.

Before everyone at the dinner table settles down, Ryder reaches behind his chair to hand me a roll.

The royals all eye their soup like hungry dogs while the food testers stand rigid, waiting the mandatory few minutes before they can declare the food safe.

Henry's food tester finally nods her head. Shoulders untense, and hands reach for spoons. The sound of metal cluttering against bowls fills the room as soon as the meal is deemed safe.

I sweep my gaze over the food display on the table, picking out whatever I hope is left after they're done. Definitely some more rolls.

Beside me, Iris, Ryder's new food tester, begins quietly wheezing. Her breaths come in short, labored bursts and she clutches a hand to her stomach.

"Are you okay?" I ask, placing a hand on her shoulder.

Just as Ryder lifts his spoon to his mouth Iris coughs with so much force she's on the ground in an instant. Every pair of eyes in the room snap to her.

She rolls onto her back to reveal blood all around her mouth. Screams erupt from different parts of the room as she starts to shake uncontrollably.

More blood bubbles out of her mouth as she moans and cries. She chokes on the thick liquid spilling from her mouth. Her eyes are wide, filled with absolute terror. Her brows pinch together as she shakes her head, wordlessly begging anything that can hear her not to let her die like this.

She pins me in her gaze, watching me with that same terror. She begs me to help her without uttering a single word.

I don't move. I don't take my eyes off her either. My feet feel like they're stuck to the ground. My heart races, making my entire body go both hot and cold at once. I want to help her. I want to do something.

But I just stand there, frozen, tears welling in my eyes as I watch her panicked expression turn from pleading to betrayal. In that fleeting moment, I see everything in her face, her fear, the hurt that I'm not moving, not doing anything to stop this. In the silence between us, her unspoken accusation cuts painfully deep.

"Someone do something!" A voice screams. Someone yells as the room fills with chaos, only barely covering the sounds of her muffled chokes until suddenly, the noise dies. She stills and the room falls into an eerie silence.

Everyone stares at her bloodied, lifeless body, until Ryder's chair stretches across the floor as he jumps up. Without a word, he grabs my arm and yanks me out of the dining room. I look over my shoulder, to see King Henry's stern eyes follow me in confusion.

"Go make yourself throw up." Ryder commands, his voice harsh. What- *the roll.*

"I think it was only in the soup-"

"Now! Please."

"Okay." I don't question him again, I just nod and speed walk down the hall to the kitchen and hurl up the small amount of food into the sink. I wipe my mouth with a groan as I wash out the sink.

As I turn around I nearly crash into Ryder, who's standing just barely behind me. He cups my face in his hands, moving my hair behind my ear to check every inch of my face.

"Are you okay? How do you feel? Do you feel strange at all?" His voice has a slight, rare tremble as his eyes scan over me on repeat.

"I'm fine," I reassure him.

"Are you sure?"

"I ate before Iris did. If there was anything in the roll I would've already died by now." His breath hitches at the end of my sentence.

"I'm so sorry." He loosens his grip on my cheeks a little, never taking his eyes off me. Even as he accepts that I'm okay he doesn't seem to relax. His brows are knit together, his eyes wide, and his breathing is deep and heavy.

"Why? You don't have any reason to be sorry. You couldn't have known."

"I should've waited until after the testers were done before I gave you anything. I'm so, so sorry, Isabelle."

I take his hands off my face and hold them in my own.

"It's okay, really. You didn't force that roll down my throat. I could've waited. It's okay, Ryder." He still doesn't look any more at ease. The weight of what could've happened is still clearly written across his face, "I doubt they will have you go straight into your after lunch tasks while they deal with this. Do you want to go down to the river before they drag you back to your 'Princely Duties'?" I ask.

He just nods, still frowning. We slip out the back door of the kitchen, moving quickly before anyone can yell for him to come back while they spend hours making sure he's okay even though a drop of food never even touched his lips.

"Oh, wait one second." I turn back around and into the kitchen to grab an apple before heading back outside. I emptied out everything in my stomach and Ryder never got to eat a single bite of lunch. I take a big crunching bite, feeling the tart sweetness of the fruit fill my mouth before handing it to Ryder.

"Here. I can be your tester," I joke, still chewing on my bite. Bile churns in my stomach with self disgust at the joke given what just happened. But I really want to be able to say something to get that look off his face. Iris's panicked expression and the sound of her gasping for air while she choked on her own blood...it was horrible. I know that right now Ryder's imagining that being me on the floor, dying, afraid, and in pain like she did.

"That's not funny, Isabelle, not funny at all. Also, it's disgusting to talk while you're eating," he mutters, not even meeting my eyes as he talks.

I roll my eyes at him while he takes his own bite out of the apple. The entire walk to the river he holds my hand extra tight, as if he's afraid to let go.

It's too early in the day for the flowers to be glowing or for the ripples of water in the river to have the extra glowing highlights of blue, but the flowers are still pretty and the sounds of the running water are as soothing as ever. The sun has warmed us up, and the water is just right to cool us down.

Ryder seems to have relaxed a bit over the walk here, but his jaw is still tight and his eyes still seem like he's not entirely present, stuck in what would've happened if he had dipped that roll in some soup first, like he often does.

His now obviously faked smile fades as he gets lost in thought, his gaze fixed on a purple fully bloomed flower. Telling him for the millionth time that I'm fine seems like a waste of time.

I really liked Iris. She was new, but the few interactions we had were really sweet. I could've seen myself becoming really good friends with her, and the image of her bloodied, motionless body still makes me queasy. But physically I'm fine.

I won't be sleeping well tonight, or for the next few nights, or maybe ever again between the coughing man still haunting my mind and now Iris, and that look of betrayal in her eyes because I couldn't get myself to snap out of it and move. But it seems very obvious that there wasn't anything bad in the roll.

I strip down to the bare minimum of layers, and before Ryder can say a word I wrap my arms around his torso and fling us both into the steady river. He shoots up to the surface with a gasp.

"What was that for?" He sputters, wiping running drops of water off his face.

"You seemed lost in your own head. Better?"

"Cold." He narrows his eyes at me, water droplets dripping over them from his hair.

"Oh, come on, it's perfectly sunny and hot outside. And if all you're thinking about is how cold you are or how rude that was for me to do, then it still worked."

This intense self disgust washes over me for behaving this way after watching someone die. But when I look back at Ryder, that feeling fades just a little.

People are owed the respect of taking a moment to acknowledge that something awful has happened when they die, but I can pay her that respect and empathy she deserves while she haunts my nightmares tonight. Right now I just want Ryder to stop feeling guilty about what could've happened.

His face softens, a ghost of a smile crossing his lips before he chews the inside of his cheek for just one second and I immediately know what's going to happen.

"Ryder..." I start, warning him off, but he's already shaking his head, that mischievous glint returning.

"You asked for this."

"No-" I sloppily splash away from him as he lunges after me dragging me under the water with him. We chase each other back and forth until my muscles are weak, the water has begun to glow, and we know that by the time we get back they'll have a search party ready for him. But for now, it doesn't matter.

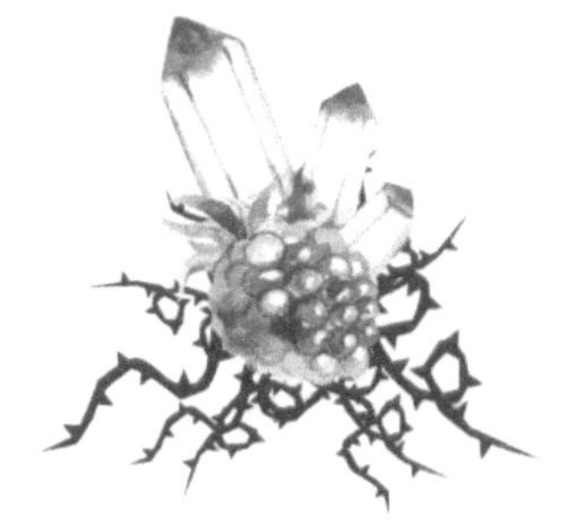

CHAPTER

II

ISABELLE

Our wet clothes cling to our skin as we make our way from the river to the ladder leading up to me and Ryder's secret spot. We don't typically ever use the ladder, even though it's much safer. Ryder looks back and forth with one hand on rungs of the ladder, ready to go, making sure there's no one around before we start climbing.

"Come on, hurry," Ryder urges, motioning his hand towards the ladder for me to go first. I pull myself up and start climbing as quickly as I can. Ryder's already climbing up right behind me.

He wanted a little bit more time before he has to deal with hours of people checking him and making a huge fuss about him, even though the soup never even touched his lips.

This happened to his dad once when Ryder and I were little. I didn't see it, but I know the food tester died and the king never even ate any of the food. Ryder said that was the day he realized how selfish so many of the royals were, and how much people idolize them as something far beyond the importance of normal people.

Growing up as my best friend, Ryder didn't see much of a difference between the royals and everyone else. In his mind, we were all just people who lived in different types of rooms, wearing different kinds of clothes. That was the day he realized most royals don't care if you live or die unless you're one of them. He didn't like that he was a part of that.

I always felt the difference, though. I always saw it, just not between us.

For the rest of the week people kept checking on his dad. They spent hours right after that checking him for any signs that he might have ingested any poison. Everyone wanted to make sure he was okay, but not a single word was said about the food tester that died right in front of everyone. Not many people seemed to care.

I think that's why Ryder doesn't want to be seen yet. He doesn't want to see people obviously care so much about someone who didn't eat a single drop of that soup, and care so little about the person who died choking on their own blood.

I will myself to please be invisible as we pass King Archer's bedroom. Every foreign royal has their own bedroom here for their stays. I have no idea if he's even in there but I'm positive it would be terrible for him to see Ryder and I out here.

I reach the last step of the ladder and plant my hand firmly on the flat surface above me then pull myself up. I let out a very unattractive and breathless grunt as my chest slams against the concrete, then roll onto my side to get myself all the way up. Going up the ladder is more painful than dangerously crawling up steep roofs. My hands hurt from gripping the metal so strongly and my shoulders burn from pulling myself up with each step.

I lie on my back for a moment while Ryder pulls himself up next to me. The dining room lies several floors beneath us and a little to the right. I can feel the weight of every-thing that happened beneath us on my back, like Iris is reminding me of what happened to her and what Ryder narrowly escaped from. I sit up and roll my shoulders, hoping I can shake the feeling away.

Ryder rolls onto his back, taking a few deep breaths, before sitting up beside me.

"Were the two of you close?" he asks.

"No, I barely knew her." She had only just started working here a couple of weeks ago, after King Henry's old food tester retired. Once any servants or palace staff that has been working here for at least ten years turn seventy, the palace pays for them to get a small house and they live off of whatever they have saved up. Most turn their house into a homestead.

Ryder nods, his hand covering mine as we stare out at the same view we've seen a million times before.

"We should go back inside. If they don't find you soon they're going to tear this place apart brick by brick." I say, pulling my hand out from under his and crawling to the other side of our secret spot so we can make our way to Ryder's room.

"They've probably already started," he mutters with a scoff. We slowly slide down each slanted roof on our butts, using our hands and feet to move ourselves along. By the time we're back in Ryder's room my palms are dotted with little bumps and bits of pebble stuck in them.

As soon as I slip through the window I head straight for the door. Nobody will have noticed that I was gone, but I'm sure his mom already assumes we were together. The next time she sees me, I would rather not be standing by his side.

"I'm going to go hang my clothes so they're dry by dinner time," I tell Ryder.

"Good idea," he says. His voice is distant as his eyes scan all around his room, obviously not also ready to leave. I walk back towards him.

"Are you okay?" I ask.

"What? Yeah–yeah, of course." He stutters. I just stare at him, waiting for him to tell the truth. He sighs and looks down.

"I don't even know her name and she died from the poison meant for me. You could've died because of my own actions if whoever did this had done something to the rolls too." He says. I grab his hand and lean my head down so he'll meet my gaze. His emerald green eyes are glazed over and laced with so much guilt.

"What happened to her is awful, but she's the food tester. The entire point of her job is that when someone tries to attack you, she, or any other food testers, will die instead. That's not your fault." I firmly tell him.

He pulls his lips in and nods, still looking guilty.

I want to stay here with him until he understands that what happened wasn't his fault. What could've happened to me wouldn't have been his fault.

Just because your actions end up leading to something doesn't always mean it's your fault. It would've happened because of whoever poisoned his food, not Ryder. If you decide not to go on a walk with someone, and they go alone then get murdered, it's not your fault. It's the murderer's fault.

But someone is bound to triple check Ryder's room soon, and if I'm still here when they do, then it's going to end badly for both of us.

"I need to go. You'll be okay. This wasn't your fault." I say, stepping away, but he grabs my hand before I can leave.

"Thank you," he says, his voice soft and fraying, then he drops my hand.

I crack open his door, poking my head out to make sure no one is around before stepping out and quickly shutting it behind me.

I drop my shoulders and let out a breath of relief once I'm a few steps away from his door. No one coming down the hall would be able to tell I was in there.

I turn left down the hall to the kitchen. The laundry room is a few doors down from there, and the clothesline is right outside the kitchen door. If I change into the laundry dress–one of the five plain white dresses all the servants wear when we have to wash our own clothes–and hang up my uniform now, it should be dry by dinner time...hopefully.

"Isabelle?" A familiar voice calls from behind me just as I'm about to take my first step down the stairs. I slowly turn around and see Queen Lunana.

I love her, and I think she loves me too, so I usually always enjoy seeing her whenever King Henry isn't around, but she must know Ryder and I were together.

"Hi, Queen Luana," I say with a weak smile, fidgeting with my fingers behind my back.

"Have you seen Ryder? We've all been looking everywhere for him since lunch, I assumed he was with you." She and Ryder make the same face when they're worried. While I feel bad that we made her worry about her son's whereabouts right after an assassination attempt, I'm relieved that she's not mad at me for being with him, especially when we both knew he was supposed to stay here.

"He's in his room," the words slip out before I can stop them. *Sorry Ryder.*

Queen Luana lets out a sigh of relief, her shoulders relax as an invisible weight lifts off of her.

"Thank you, sweetheart," she says, weakly waving a hand and then turning away. I head back to the stairs but out of the corner of my eyes I see her turn back towards me before she's even taken a second step towards Ryder's room.

"Are you okay?" she asks me, this time looking worried in a completely different way.

"I'm okay." I nod. I am, but she has a way of making me feel so raw and exposed when she looks at me like that and asks if I'm okay. It makes me wanna crawl in her lap and cry.

"Did you two know each other well?" She asks tenderly. Her face falling into a sympathetic expression.

"No, I only ever talked to her once," I reply. It was when she first started working as Ryder's food tester and her sister was introducing her to everyone.

"Oh," She pauses for a moment, "Henry was wondering why Ryder would leave with a servant. I told him he wanted to demonstrate care for his people for the sake of gaining loyalty."

I nod. It's amazing to me that they're genuinely in love. The two of them are such vastly different people.

"Isabelle, if you do decide that you're not okay even though you didn't know her, I don't even think I'm okay, then you can talk to me too. Whenever you need to." She looks at me with a sympathetic smile.

"Thank you, Queen Luana," I say, holding back tears. Having someone who's not your parent care for you like they are is so tender and it doesn't always feel nice. I appreciate and love her so, so much but feeling loved out of pity is like being seen in such a raw, vulnerable way and it's like being stripped of any protection to fit under someone else's. She nods and walks away towards Ryder's room.

When I think about my future the main thing that comes to mind is that nothing will change but the fact Ryder will be gone and I'll be alone. But that's not entirely true.

Queen Luana will always be here. We don't talk often and I don't expect that to change, but she really does care about me—even if it may mostly be out of pity for the fact that my mom is gone—and I care about her too.

Plus Liam will be staying here since he'll be king. We don't talk often and frankly we don't know each other as well as we should considering that his brother and I have been best friends our whole lives. But he knows I exist, which is better than nothing.

I'll be lonely, but not entirely alone.

I make it down to the servants hall. It's like the hidden source of everything we do for the royals that they don't have to watch. I quickly step towards the kitchen, ready to get this wet one piece jumper off of my skin but I slow down at the faint sound of soft cries.

I poke my head around the door frame and see Iris's sister crying on one of the stools, cradling her sister's cat. She wasn't supposed to have one here. We all just pretended we didn't notice the little kitty paw print made out of flour across the kitchen some mornings.

"Reina?" I whisper, slowly walking through the door. She stiffens up, sniffling a few times as she hastily wipes her cheeks.

"I'm so sorry," I say and wrap an arm around her. She holds a small strain of composure for as long as she can before completely breaking down, sobbing against me. I can't even begin to imagine what she must be feeling right now. I timidly hold the back of her head with one hand, rubbing large circles on her back with the other.

She just sobs and sobs while I hold her. The little orange cat looks up at us, having no idea that her person, who she follows around every day, is never coming back.

"No one even cares," she cries, her voice high and weak. "No one even cares that she died—that someone died. All everyone's been saying is 'Thank God it wasn't the important one.' She was my sister, and people are glad she died because it wasn't that *prince*." She sucks in a deep breath through gritted teeth, still sobbing, breathing too fast and too heavily.

"I'm–I'm the one who got her the job. She was going to–she wanted to be a nurse, because no one was able to help our dad when we were kids and he got sick. She was going to help people and she needed to save some money for training. I told her she–that she could come here and save up a lot of money for one year as a food tester. She was going to help people. She had so much to do, she was a whole person but no one even cares that she died horribly because it's her job so it doesn't fucking matter."

I look down at her lap and see the cat pawing at her stomach. Maybe now he knows something's wrong, maybe he's wondering where Iris is.

"Our mom's gonna be devastated." She grips onto me even tighter, soaking my jumper with her sobs. Has anyone even checked on her while everyone else was looking for Ryder?

"I'm so, so sorry, Reina." I whisper, resting my cheek on the top of her head. I just hold onto her while we cry.

The cat hops off her lap and walks out the door heading right towards Iris's room, where he won't ever find her.

"I got her the job," she repeats, her voice cracks and her sobs deepen.

"It's not your fault, it's not your fault," I repeat the same words over and over again while softly running my hand over her head. Her entire body shakes under the weight of the loss and guilt she's feeling.

We stay like this until she's sobbed as much as her body can and eventually, she passes out in my arms. I don't think she'll be sleeping so easily for a very long time. Neither one of us will. But I'll have my best friend to help, she's just lost hers.

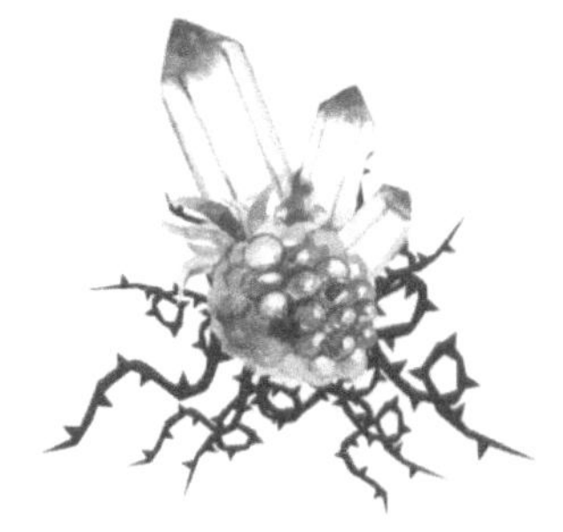

Chapter 12

Isabelle

I was right about not being able to sleep tonight. I've been trying for hours by now and every time I close my eyes, the things I imagine make me feel like I'm about to throw up. The worst of it is when everything is okay for long enough that I can start to slip into a sleeping state. Then my mind really takes over.

For days, every time I sleep I'm plagued with images of all the ways I could have helped that man and the memory of what happened when I didn't.

Maybe if I hadn't been looking around for who threw the first rock and had just gone up to help him instead, I could've shielded him. I should've pushed through the crowd harder. I should have yelled louder.

It's excruciating.

But now the ghost of that nameless man has a friend. I know there isn't anything I could have done to prevent what happened to Iris.

She's the tester.

There is no tester for the tester, and when that day comes that someone really has tried to poison a royal, then people with Iris's job are just out of luck, no matter how awful it is.

I know it, but I don't feel it.

When she was dying on the floor all I did was stand there. I'm not a doctor and putting my hand on her back or pretending I could've helped wouldn't have changed anything.

But her ghost, my own mind, still crucifies me for it. The moment her face shifted from fear and pain to betrayal because no one was moving to help her, including me, haunts me every time I shut my eyes. All I can think about is how sorry I am. Sorry to Iris, sorry to Reina, sorry to that old man whose name I didn't even know.

The guilt is paired with a crippling fear so deep it paralyzes me. That man in the village died because Dominant Point was pushing people to be that afraid. This wasn't just because of the virus, Dominant Point did this to him and no one knows it. And it's going to keep happening to millions of more people because of them.

Whoever killed Iris was trying to kill my best friend. His spoon was less than an inch from his mouth. *He* was less than an inch from death. I would've watched my best friend, my person, die writhing in pain too quickly for anyone to save him. One inch away, and it would have been his blood soaked face and choking gasps that I can't get out of my head instead of Iris's.

Whoever poisoned his food was in the palace and likely still is. They could be under the same roof as Ryder right now. But they would be stupid to try to kill him tonight, right?

Poison is anonymous. Sneaking into someone's room to kill them is guaranteed to get you caught.

Maybe I should just sleep in Ryder's room again tonight. I typically fall asleep a lot easier and the nightmares aren't as bad when I'm with him. And if I'm with him I'll know he's safe.

I wiggle my upper body to face away from the wall. As soon as my eyes focus my heart stops and nearly leaps up and out of my throat. Someone, far too big to be Ryder, just walked into my room.

I don't move. I don't speak. I don't even breathe for a whole terrifying two seconds. My heart goes from deathly still to beating so rapidly all I hear is my pulse racing like a voice in my ear.

"Isabelle." The voice grabs my shoulders, shaking me, clearly not being able to see my widely opened eyes. My heart slows just enough to process the voice.

"King Archer?"

"Get up!" He nudges me. "You have to go. Now!"

I sit up, only enough for my blanket to pool around my waist.

"What-what are you talking about? What's going on?" I force the last part of my sentence out through a yawn. He tightens both hands on my shoulders.

"You need to get out of bed and pack whatever you absolutely need. *Right now.*" I'm fully awake now and no less confused.

"Pack? Why? I'm not doing anything until you tell me what's going on." I shake my head, still not moving. He lets out a strained breath, aggravated by my perfectly understandable confusion.

"Barrett and the rest of Dominant Point have put a kill order on both you and Ryder under the claims of leaked classified information. Get up. Pack. I'll explain more while you do, quickly."

I stumble into action, pulling myself out of my tangled mess of blankets and grabbing my few possessions from under the bed.

"That's what happened at lunch today?" Another much, much worse idea comes to my mind. "His family is going along with this?" If it's an official order and Archer knows about it then his family must know too.

"No, they don't know about this. The royals have to work through the approval of Dominant Point, not the other way around."

I stop sorting through my things and turn to look at him.

"If they don't know about this then how do you?"

"I'll only explain if you keep packing. I got an anonymous letter telling me to check Barret's recent contacts with Dominant Point. I had someone from home look into it."

An anonymous letter? Who would be able to know something was going to happen unless they were a part of it? Maybe someone from Dominant Point grew a soul.

"So no one else knows?"

"Are you done packing yet?" he asks, impatiently. I lift up my medium sized fully stuffed bag over my shoulders. Without a word he strides hastily towards my door to leave.

I start to follow him but turn back around. "Wait, one more second."

I run into my bathroom and grab a fist full of pads. The ones they give the servants are itchy and leak, so Ryder just takes a whole bunch from his moms supply for me. I shove them in my bag, toss it back over my shoulder, and follow King Archer out the door.

"No, no one else knows." He says, his voice quiet but firm.

"Where am I going? What about Ryder? Why are you helping me?"

He holds my hand, pulling me through the dark hallways to Ryder's room, which I'm sure I know better than he does.

"I'll explain where you're going after we get Ryder so I don't have to do this twice. You two are going together." he says, slightly out of breath from his fast strides through the halls.

Finally hearing something about what's going to happen for Ryder lifts a part of the boulder sitting on my lungs away. A thousand half formed questions swirl at the tip of my tongue until we reach Ryder's door.

He holds my hand a few seconds longer than I expect before letting go and raising his hand to knock. Without a word, I push down his arm and gently open the door that I know is always unlocked.

The moonlight shining through his window shows the silhouette of a peaceful, sleeping Ryder. Now we're here to ruin that.

"Ryder, Ryder, wake up." I shake his shoulder, earning only a groan in response.

"Isabelle?" He doesn't open his eyes, just lifts the blanket to let me under.

"Ryder, get up."

"What's wro-" His barely opened eyes snap wide once they land on King Archer. "Archer? What are you doing here?" He looks back at me. "What's going on?"

"I know it's confusing but get up, pack only what you absolutely need, and he'll explain while you do."

"Okay." There isn't a moment of hesitation in his response or in the time it takes for him to get out of bed and move towards his closet. He's doing so much better at this than I did.

He looks back over his shoulder to King Archer with his hand ready to open his closet.

"You have five minutes for this to make sense. If you stutter, stumble, or don't adequately explain what's going on or what I'm packing for by then, you get out and apologize to Isabelle for involving her in this."

With that, he pulls open the closet door and disappears inside.

To my own surprise, by the end of what has probably been five minutes he's explained the gist of the situation and he did it much better than he did to me, even with all my questions. I feel kind of like a testing dummy.

"Why are you helping us?" Ryder asks, his voice sharp as he looks at King Archer.

"Well, I'm not going to let two kids be murdered over some gossip."

"Do you know what it is that they are willing to kill us for to remain a secret?"

"Not at all, and for the love of God, don't tell me." Ryder eases up on his interrogation, still seeming only somewhat satisfied.

"What's your plan?" Ryder asks.

"I have a safe location for you two to go." Archer looks around Ryder at the star-lit black sky. "We need to go. I'll explain the rest while we move." I perk up and butt into their tense conversation.

"You're coming with us?" I ask.

"Absolutely not. I'm the King. I can't just leave. I meant that I'll explain while we move to get outside and *you two* go."

"Oh." I don't know him very well and after lunch the other day he makes me a little uncomfortable. But he knows more about what's going on than Ryder and I do and he clearly wants us to be safe.

King Archer takes long strides to the door, followed by Ryder, and lastly me. I look back into Ryder's room to glance at the elaborately carved clock that until now I had forgotten about. It's around two o'clock. Once we're a few paces past the door Ryder steps back a bit to lock his hand in mine.

"Are you okay?" he asks with a light squeeze of my hand as we hurriedly follow Archer down the hall. I nod.

"Are you okay?" I ask back. There have only been a handful of times when I've asked that question and gotten an honest answer when it was no. I don't expect this to be one of those times, at least not while Archer is right in front of us.

"I'm fine." Ryder pulls me back when I almost go down the wrong hall.

"You're going the wrong way," I whisper-shout to Archer. "The closest way outside is down the other hall."

"I'm not taking you the fastest way. You're going out of the kitchen so you can grab a few days worth of food. Just stuff that can stay good in a pack for a while. Jerky, nuts, nothing very good."

"A few days? Where are we going?" Ryder asks. King Archer seems to have some kind of personal dislike towards explaining crucial information.

"You're going to my uncle's house. He died several years ago and no one has lived there since then. It's a homestead and it's far away from the nearest town, so no one will recognize Ryder. Since I wasn't born a royal, no one knows anything about my family. They have no reason to care, so no one, including Dominant Point, knows about it."

"How do we get there?" Ryder asks.

My mind completely drowns out of the present moment, the reality of this suddenly sinking in. The collective government wants us dead, I'm leaving the only place I have ever known as home, and the idea creeps up my spine and into the deepest part of my mind that there's a good chance it will never be safe to come back.

Dominant Point isn't likely to just say 'no worries' and trust us to keep this secret to ourselves. We'll be spending the rest of our lives in this dead uncle's house.

And that whole 'rest of our lives' may not even be very long. This is *Dominant Point*.

They're the leading power over every single stretch of land in the world. They're not exactly running low on resources and if they want someone dead then without a doubt they can make it happen.

An unnerving memory from my mom's journal pops into my head. She said Dominant Point has technology unlike anything we've ever even heard of, even beyond the royals.

While the citizens are still using candle sticks, palaces have light switches. Of course, many palaces still use candles just for style purposes or in areas they don't care to change like the servants quarter.

The royals have plenty of technology that the rest of the people don't, but what Dominant Point has is supposed to be unimaginable. She wrote that it seemed like something completely out of place in this world.

If they have the kind of technology that's just so beyond what we're used to, surely they have something that can help them find us.

"Are you absolutely sure they won't find us at your uncle's house?" I ask, only now realizing that Archer explained how to get to the house so thoroughly that Ryder has no more questions.

"Yes. No one knows about it because it was never important, not even my wife." I nod, chewing my lip before leaning into Ryder's ear.

"Where did he say the house was?" I whisper.

"The northeast side of Adhara. We should be able to make it in a week if we take minimal breaks," he whispers back.

"You know how to get there just from him saying 'northeast'?"

"No. He gave me the coordinates to mark on my map and some land mars to look for when we get closer. Were you listening?"

"No," I whisper.

"That's okay."

We reach the kitchen, and Archer keeps watch while we collect any food good for a week long journey. Well, I do. Ryder hardly knows where anything is unless it's one of our go-to late night snacks.

We have apples and bananas for the first couple of days, lots and lots of jerky, and nut mix. Turns out, not many royals want to jerky when they could have gourmet meals with a delicacy for every course instead, so it's mostly for servants to snack on throughout the day.

"Is this enough?" I ask as Ryder scoops up food to put in his bag.

"Yes. If we ration and make good time, then we should have enough food for everyday." As Ryder zips up his bag King Archer pushes open the back door. He motions his head outside, probably not wanting to say, 'let's go' for the millionth time.

The moment we walk out the door Ryder seems content to keep walking without any more time wasted, satisfied with his knowledge of where we're going, why, and how much food we have.

I'm just about to follow after him, a little shell shocked that it's really happening now, when Archer grabs my shoulder and turns me to face him.

"Be careful." He stares at me for another moment, something I don't quite recognize, etching the lines of his face, before he goes back inside and locks the door behind him. When I turn back around Ryder is right by my side.

He takes my hand in his and strokes tiny circles on the backside of my palm. "Are you okay?"

"Yeah."

"Okay." He gives my hand a light squeeze. "Let's go."

CHAPTER 13

ISABELLE

"I'm surprised you weren't more hesitant. You went along with it pretty quickly." I say to Ryder.

We've been walking for about half an hour now. Ryder and I have never needed to fill the silence when we were together, we could just be quiet and be glad to be around each other. But right now, I really don't want to be quiet. I don't want to give myself the time to think.

"I was hesitant at first, but everything he said made sense. The only thing that doesn't is how Barret found out that we knew. But that could've happened any number of ways. He could've found your moms journal if he thought you were acting differently and searched your room to figure out why. Or he could've overheard you and I talking about it.

"And there's no doubt that if Dominant Point found out that we knew, they wouldn't just let it go. It also makes sense with you saying that you heard him whisper-shouting at someone and then he got mad at you. One, he may have been angry when talking to the other person because he was stressed about the order he was going to give. Two, he's always been nice to you and him snapping at you is extremely out of character unless he knew something."

"Oh." Duh.

"Did you not believe him?" Ryder asks, turning towards me with a raised brow.

"No, I did. I just figured you wouldn't. You're in a constant state of being skeptical of anything anyone says to you ever."

He laughs a probably forced laugh. He hasn't let go of my hand since we first started walking, and the silent reassurance of us both being here together is probably the one thing keeping me grounded.

He shifts to look back at the palace and suddenly the reassurance in my hand is gone. He's down on one knee in front of his bag, pulling something out.

"What are you doing?" I ask.

"We're finally far away enough from the palace and in an area bright enough for me to do this." He pulls out a map of Adhara and traces a few invisible lines on the sheet before settling on a specific point and marking it with his pencil. He then marks a bunch of other spots around it. The only light to guide his movements comes from the stars and moonlight filtering between the tree branches.

"This is where his uncle's house is." He points to the largest dot he drew.

"And the doodles around it?"

"Different landmarks to look out for." He carefully folds the map and slips it back into his bag, throwing it over his shoulder to keep walking. I bite my lip with the heavy words sitting right on the tip of my tongue.

"I'm sorry," I blurt out. Ever since I pushed open the door to his room next to King Archer I've felt the weight of my guilt in every muscle.

"For what?" He turns towards me, his expression a mix of confusion and concern.

"For telling you about this. For getting you involved and taking away the rest of your life. I'm so, so sorry, Ryder."

He tugs on my hand, stopping me in my tracks, then braces his hands on my shoulders.

"This is not your fault. Before you showed me the journal, you warned me it might be better if I didn't know. You gave me plenty of warning, and it was my choice. I chose to read that journal, even after you warned me. You didn't drag me to this point. I chose it." He says firmly, gently shaking my shoulders like it'll get the point across even more.

But all I can think about are the plans he had for his life, the future that's now slipping away to live in hiding.

"I'm so sorry."

"I'm not mad at you." He repeats.

"*How?* The rest of your life is ruined because of what I showed you. You were gonna travel all across the world, see every beautiful thing it has to offer. You were going to make a real difference. Now you're going to spend the rest of your life in some dead uncle's house with me, because of me."

My voice cracks as my throat tightens. It feels like every day I have something new to be sorry for, and nothing that I can make right. He pulls me into a tight hug, tucking my head under his chin.

"I was going to spend the rest of my life as a part of the horrible group leading and abusing the world." He states, his voice laced with disgust.

"But you would've had so much, maybe you could've changed it. I'm so, so sorry for taking that away from you." Ryder pulls me out of the hug to cup my face in his hands.

"You took nothing away from me. Don't feel guilty about any of this, not for a second. I mean it. There's not even the slightest part of me that blames you or holds any ill will towards you. I chose to have you show me what was in the journal, despite your warnings." He pulls me back into a hug, running a soothing hand over the back of my head and the lumps of my braid. "Okay?"

"Okay." I muffle the words against his chest, sinking into the steady rhythm of his heartbeat.

"Good. Then let's keep going." He takes the next step, slipping his hand back into mine.

Leaves and twigs snap beneath our feet every few steps, and despite knowing there's no one around it still feels wrong to even breathe too loudly.

Of all the months the government could have decided they want us dead they chose a pretty nice one for us. It's just under a month until summer so the nights aren't too cold. It was so hot during the day that now the air just feels cozy.

We passed the river a little while ago but we're still close enough to hear the water rushing by behind us. The same water we played in together just a few hours ago.

It's hard to imagine that the memory of us splashing around in the river was this same day. It feels wrong that these two entirely different experiences could be so close together.

"Maybe– I was thinking that once we're safe, we could maybe try to find my mom," I say. Ryder's hand briefly clenches in mine. "I was just thinking that if she's managed to stay hidden for this long she must've had help, right? She wrote in her journal that she had gone to Dominant Point to see a friend...maybe that friend helped her out.

"And Archer said that his uncle's house is far away from the nearest town, maybe her friend found a place like that for her too, maybe even sort of near us." I say, growing more and more hopeful with each word. He's quiet for a moment. I know what he's thinking and that hopefulness starts to flicker and fade.

"Just because it doesn't seem like we'll have anything better to do anyway." I say, trying to brush off that painful feeling of faded hope. Another stretch of silence fills the space between us.

"If you would like to try finding her I will be by your side every step of the way, but I don't want you to get your hopes up. If she's managed to stay hidden from Dominant Point, with all of their resources and power…it's unlikely we'll be the ones to find her." Ryder says, his voice soft but steady.

"I understand that." He's right. It's very unlikely we'll find her, and that should be the hard truth I have to swallow. But as I glance over at him I can feel the unspoken words lingering between us. He probably thinks she's dead.

"We won't walk for much longer. We can set up camp for the rest of the night then keep going in the morning. Just a couple more miles." He says, obviously changing topics. I nod, unsure if he's even looking my way as I drag my tired feet over the forest floor.

We only walk for another hour, maybe two at most. But by the time we're done it's still pitch black, without even the smallest sliver of light creeping over the horizon.

"Okay, I think we can stop here until morning," he says. I don't say anything. I just nod, my body heavy and weak as I drop to my knees to pull my blanket out of my bag. His hand rests on my shoulder from behind me.

"Are you okay?" he asks softly.

I nod again, "Mhm, just tired," I mumble.

He lightly squeezes my shoulder, then turns back to his bag. The spot he picked for us is a small, circle-ish area in the trees, with just enough space for us to spread out. The ground is covered with lush grass, and the faint sining of night time bugs and animals are the only sounds around us.

He lays his blanket down across from me then props his elbows on his knees, watching me lay my blanket down and fold half of it over myself while I lay on top of the other half, trying to make this as comfortable as I can.

"It's going to be okay." Ryder says, in that steady calm voice that could make you believe getting mauled by a bear will be okay.

"I know." *We* will be okay. I know we'll be safe once we get to King Archer's uncle's house. I even get part of what I've wanted my whole life, to stay with my best friend. But it comes at the cost of billions of people dying.

We'll be okay, no one else will.

"When we–" A twig snaps somewhere around us. We freeze, peering through the darkness for where the sound could've come from. I squint into the distance, trying to make out any shapes between the trees. I turn back to Ryder and see him pressing his finger to his lips, silently telling me not to make a sound.

It's quiet for long enough that I can imagine all the sounds I should be terrified of hearing. Boots stomping on the forest floor as Dominant Point finds us, the growl of a hungry animal, anything that could live in the dark, quiet woods around us.

Ryder slowly moves his finger away from his lips and eases his shoulders just a bit. I let out a breath, feeling my heart finally start to slow down. It could've just been an animal, hopefully the kind that doesn't eat people.

"It's–" More snapping sounds get closer. I look back and forth, unable to tell which direction it's coming from. The snapping twigs and heavy steps get closer as an awful groaning sound gets louder.

The groaning and snapping sounds of branches and leaves beneath someone's feet gets closer and closer until a man with bloody, teary eyes stumbles in front of us and then collapses to the ground between us. His skin is covered in bruises and his hands are frantically moving all across his skin, like he's trying to get something off or out of him.

"Please, please, please," the man on the ground begs, his voice trembling as he sobs. He trembles and shakes as the bruises grow with each passing second.

A crystal splits out of his skin from his stomach, dragging down a few inches before it stops. The man's hands hover over the wound, his eyes locked on the unnatural sight with pure horror. He screams with wide eyes staring at what was splitting him open.

Ryder grabs me by my arm and pulls hard.

"Isabelle, we have to go now, he's sick!" he yells through the fabric of his shirt, which he's holding over his mouth with his other hand.

He pulls me until I snap back into the moment. Pure fear and energy jolt through my body, sending me into motion and running beside him.

I look over my shoulder at the sick man on the floor. He screams so loud with his hands still hovering over the crystal stuck in place in his stomach. Then, the screams come to a sudden stop. A tiny, much smaller crystal sticks out of his neck. I listen to him choke and gurgle on his own blood, some splattering out of his neck. Then he's completely silent.

Oh my God.

Ryder pulls me along by my hand as I stumble over my own feet. Every panicked breath feels like blades in my lungs, a sharp reminder of the crystals that just tore him apart from the inside out. He holds onto my hand tightly, practically dragging me behind him.

I don't know how far we ran, or how long we've walked until Ryder finally says we can stop again. I didn't even know if we had grabbed our stuff before leaving until I felt my blanket being draped over my shoulders.

All I know is that Dominant Point isn't just killing people. Dominant Point is doing *that* to people, to children.

I keep thinking about how they're able to have enough power to do this to people, and it seems obvious that no one group should hold as much power as they do. But there aren't really any good systems either.

I had actually liked the idea of Dominant Point up until recently. There's no war, no hatred based on where someone is from, it's like every kingdom is holding hands.

When every kingdom was separate, there was too much division. There was tension between each kingdom at almost any given moment and they were free to abuse and mistreat their people however they wanted. Sometimes it was hatred for people from other kingdoms, sometimes it was for groups of their own people.

Dominant Point brought the world together. No more systemic racism or sexism. We all worked to build each other up, to make life better for everyone everywhere. It was no longer us against them. Any resources that a kingdom had, which once would've sparked a war, were now shared across the world. Humanity as a team, not a division.

The world flourished, at first.

But it's a small group of people responsible for the whole world. They get greedy and selfish. They decide that even though they exist for the people, suddenly they actually exist to make the people live as the leaders want, not for what's actually best for the people they were sworn to protect.

Dominant Point is killing people brutally just for the sake of making extra sure they remain in power, but I don't know if that's really so much worse than the things we did to each other when we were separated.

Or maybe it is. At least when each separate kingdom was mass murdering others and their own, they claimed to have a set of beliefs around it.

There shouldn't be seven people dictating the lives and well being of billions of people, but nearly every government system there could possibly be, leads to something awful after enough time.

What Dominant Point is doing is for their own power alone. And because they don't want to give that up, people just need to die.

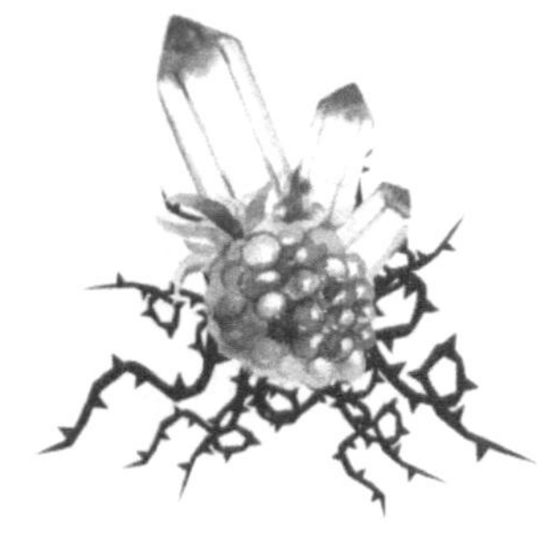

CHAPTER 14

ISABELLE

The air smells fresher than I may have ever smelled it. The sun shines on my skin just enough to feel cozy. And, embarrassingly, I think I drooled.

I stretch my limbs out before ever opening my eyes, and the moment I do, our reality crashes back into me.

"Sleep well?" Ryder asks, already up and alert. We walked for a few hours last night before taking a bit of time to rest. By now, the palace is just a speck in the distance.

I nod, rubbing my eyes as I sit up.

"How long do you think we've been stopped?" I ask.

"About four hours," he says without hesitation. I look over and see the sundial he's placed in the dirt. "It should be a little past eight. Are you ready to get going?"

I nod again, yawning as Ryder kicks apart any sign of us having rested here.

"We'll walk for about three and a half hours, take a short break, and repeat that three times before setting up camp for tonight. Does that sound okay?" he asks.

Throughout all of this, he hasn't appeared to be lost in any way for even a second. Forever the prince, trained to handle every serious situation with grace and ease. He's like a diplomatic shell of himself. It's the same way he changes when his father is around.

"That's fine," I agree.

The sun drifts across the sky as we walk. Sometimes we talk about plans, sometimes we talk about unimportant things, sometimes we don't talk at all.

I can't stop thinking about the man from last night. Every bunny that shuffles in a bush has me looking over my shoulder, waiting for someone else to die horribly.

I still know that what the people in town did to the man who only coughed was terrible—something no human being should be capable of doing to someone who never tried to hurt them. But if those people had already seen what it looks like to die from this disease, then no wonder they were so terrified.

I wonder if the man from last night had already seen this happen to others. Maybe it was his family, his kids, and he knew what was going to happen to him. Maybe he got lucky and was the first person in his town or village to get sick.

We just sat down for our first short break and my legs are already killing me.

"Are you ready to keep going?" Ryder asks as he brings himself to his feet.

"Wow, you weren't kidding when you said 'short break'." I run my hands over my knees, giving my legs a silent pep talk for the hours ahead.

"Our chances of avoiding being found by Dominant Point at any point get much better the moment we reach his uncle's house. We also don't have enough rations to extend this trip to our leisure." His calm and collected demeanor only shows how much more panicked he is than he's letting on. Anytime he's been really afraid of something or hurt he slips into this state of being only exactly what he was trained to be.

Everything he does is calculated and thought through, only because he's terrified of what'll happen if he's not.

I dust the salty residue of the nut mix off my hands.

"Sorry."

"Don't be," he replies, shaking his head. "We just need to keep the breaks short."

"Okay." A grunt escapes my lips as I stand up. Why do muscles always wait to really hurt until after they've had a moment to rest? Ryder drops his bag down one arm and swings it around so it hangs in front of him.

"What are you doing?" I ask. He turns his back to me, holds his hands out behind him, and leans down.

"Get on." He nods his head towards himself.

"What?"

"You're tired, and we have to get moving." He opens his hands wider to emphasize his point. I lift one leg to the side of his waist, drape my arms loosely around his neck, then pull up the other leg.

"Comfortable?" he asks, his mouth right next to my ear, as he pulls me up higher.

"Are you sure this is a good idea? You're going to get tired faster." I point out. He scoffs and starts walking.

Each step he takes bounces me up and down. "We are going to be passing by a town today. We'll keep our distance, but I think that if there aren't too many people it would be good to get a little more food and fill up our water. We'll have our masks so as long as it's fairly empty we shouldn't be noticed. After we pass, it'll be a while before we come across another populated area. Does that sound okay?" he asks.

"That's fine." Both words dig my chin into the crook of his neck. My head bounces up and down on his shoulder with each step. He digs through the bag hanging on his front and pulls out two squares of fabric, then hands one to me.

"Tie this around your head to cover your mouth once we get to town."

"Okay." I tuck it between my chin and his shoulder until I need it. From this close, I can see the faint dusting of freckles over his cheeks that I rarely notice. His unfairly thick, black eye lashes frame his emerald green eyes, made even brighter by the sun shining down on us.

"Are you worried about your family?" I ask, watching him as he stares straight ahead.

"They don't know about the origin of the sickness, Dominant Point won't go after them."

"I'm not talking about them getting hurt," I clarify. He lifts my legs higher on his waist before speaking.

"I'm worried about how my mother and brother are. I'm sure they've realized I'm gone by now, and it may take Liam a while to really be worried, but I can't imagine how my mother must be feeling. A part of me hopes Archer will tell her I've left with you, not why, just that I'm safe. But I also understand that wouldn't be safe and he won't do it."

"Maybe after we get settled and safe we can find a way to tell her that you're okay," I say, my chin still digging uncomfortably into his shoulder.

"That's a nice thought, but we can't do that. We can't risk it." He's right, just like he was right about our chances of finding my mom. Reaching out to her wouldn't just put us in danger–it could make her a target as well. I want to force some hope or optimism down his throat, even if it's for unrealistic things. I rest my head over his shoulder, my check against his.

"Are we going to try to find you a cat?" he asks, I feel the movement of each word against my face.

"What?"

"A few years ago you told me that if you ever stopped being a servant the first thing you were going to do is get a pet, most likely a cat. I assume that will be our first priority once we're there?"

"Of-" Ryder drops us to the ground.

"What's going on?"

"Look." He gestures his head to the road on the other side of the trees.

It's three of the Adhara cars. Unless it's for something important, they typically use carriages, and as of yesterday there was nothing scheduled.

"Look in the middle car." Ryder points down my line of vision.

"Liam? Why would he be out here? These things are scheduled weeks in advance."

"I don't know." He brings himself to an upward crouched position and holds his hand out for me. "Him being out here could be related to our disappearance. We'll see what we can find out from a distance. This shouldn't take us off our plan if we're quick."

Ryder holds my hand as we step through the forest lining the road, moving carefully until the car stops at the edge of town.

Liam steps out of the middle car, a fabric mask covering his face, and starts helping the servants and guards accompanying him as they unload supplies.

"Why would Liam come to give the town aid?" I ask. That's something royals do from the comfort of their lavish beds after giving the order for it to be done by someone else.

"I doubt my parents are aware of this, definitely not my father. He probably snuck out at the last minute to help." he says in a hushed tone, not quite a whisper.

A very Liam thing to do.

No matter how insensitive it may seem that he manages to find humor in nearly everything, he's a softy with a big, open heart. Most of the supplies are medicine, water, blankets, and food like large bags of rice and fruit.

He passes bags of supplies down an assembly line of palace staff and some directly to the townspeople from a distance. Now that I'm actually looking at them, none of them seem to be doing very well.

Liam reaches back for another bag to pass down the line only for his hand to land on the bare surface of that empty cart.

He shouts something inaudible from our position to the rest of the staff, then walks towards a full cart tucked behind a building, away from the rest of the town.

"We can go now. He's just here to pass out supplies." Ryder stands up beside me and I yank him back down.

"Look." I point.

As Liam lifts two large bags of rice over his shoulder, a man in a dark gray mask covering his head approaches him from behind. Liam seems completely unaware of the man taking soft steps up behind him.

Right as Ryder starts to settle down behind the bushes shielding us from view, he shoots back up when a flash of silver pokes out from behind the masked man's back—a knife. The man pulls the blade all the way out and grips it firmly in his hand as he quickens his steps towards Liam.

"Ryder, wait–"

"Stay here, don't move!" He urges me as he runs down the hill toward his brother.

The moment Liam's eyes land on Ryder he freezes. The masked man momentarily stops as well before picking up his steps to Liam. Liam lifts his hand over his eyes as if his brother may be an illusion from the sun.

"Ryder? Where the hell-" The masked man grabs Liam by the shoulder, spinning him around with his other arm raised and the knife gleaming in his hand.

Liam freezes and before the would-be assassin can move the knife even two inches towards Liam's throat, Ryder throws himself onto him, bringing them both to the ground.

I shoot up to my feet and stumble over myself a bit in my attempt to make it down the hill in time to help. Within seconds, Ryder has the man in a headlock, tightening his grip around his neck.

The masked man struggles, swinging his body back and forth in an attempt to get out of Ryder's grasp. He furiously hits Ryder's arms wrapped around his neck and reaches up to hit and scratch at Ryder's face. His movements slow until he's completely still. I make it to them right as he drops his limbs completely. Liam is the first to speak.

"What, the honest to God, *fuck?* Where have you been? Why were you already here? Did you know someone was going to kill me? Mom practically had a heart attack when they told her no one knew where you were."

"Liam," Ryder stands up and dusts off his pants. "Stop talking. He's going to wake up soon." Liam's face sombers as his eyes land on his would-be murderer.

"Oh." He says, looking back at the sleeping man with a new seriousness drawn across his face.

"Oh, what?" I ask, unsure of whatever silent message they've gotten across to each other. Both their eyes land on me. Liam puts his hands on his hips and looks up to the sky, while Ryder takes my hand.

"You should get back to our trail, we'll be there in a minute." Ryder nods his head toward the trees.

"What? Why?"

"What trail? What are you guys doing?" Liam and I ask him at the same time. Ryder completely ignores his brother and keeps his eyes on me.

"He's going to wake up soon. We can't allow him to be able to tell them where he saw us or, worse, follow us. You should go back to our path, we'll be there soon."

"But-"

"Please, Isabelle." His eyes have a pleading look in them that makes me reluctantly drop his hand and step back.

"Okay." I agree.

"Seriously, what the hell is up with you guys? You've been missing all day." I don't answer Liam and neither does Ryder. As I walk back up the hill to our path, I look back over my shoulder and see Ryder pick up a rock. I make sure not to turn around again until I know I won't see them through the trees. I sped up my steps up the hill, understanding why they wanted me to leave.

I hear twigs snap behind me then Liam's voice.

"Are you sure? If we leave now he won't follow us."

"Yes, I'm sure," Ryder says, quieter. The only way I can identify the sound that comes next is that it sounds exactly like what happened to the old man, except without any cries or begging. The hauntingly familiar bash of skull into his flesh and brain.

Only this one never got the chance to be as afraid.

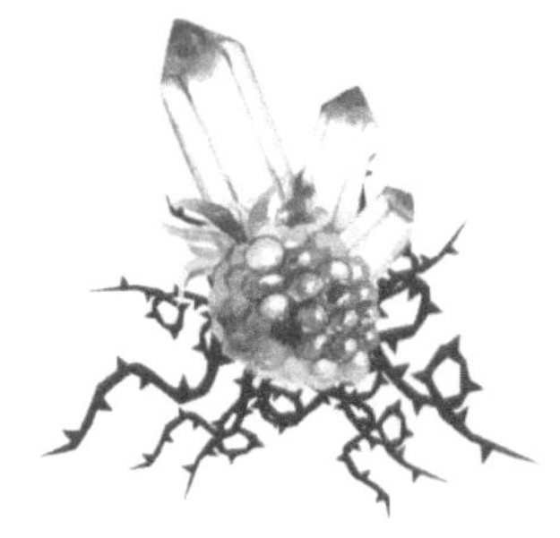

CHAPTER 15

ISABELLE

I sit over my feet with my knees to my chest, running my fingers through the blades of grass. It's easy enough to guess why there was an assassination attempt on Liam directly after Ryder. They are brothers so it makes sense that Dominant Point would've assumed that Ryder had told Liam about what we knew.

They clearly don't do enough research because Ryder never shares anything with Liam.

Sticks and leaves crunch behind me under the weight of the two boys as they approach me.

"Are you ready to keep going, or would you like to stop for a few minutes?" Ryder's eyes scan me as if he has any reason to believe I would be hurt. I've seen someone die before, three times actually. I don't want to see or hear that ever again, but coddling me like I can't handle it but he can is just annoying.

"No, we can go now." I stand up and look a bit closer at him as I do. There are splotches of blood on his shoe, his hands are smeared in it, likely rubbed onto the dark fabric of his pants. Tiny freckles of blood are splattered on one side of his cheek. Nausea starts to form in my stomach at the idea of what I know just happened before Liam interrupts me.

"Keep going where? I'm going home. In case you forgot, someone tried to *kill me,* which you guys are being way too normal about. I mean, let's take a moment at least. I'm having cake and a warm bath. Also, you guys need to come home too. Like, now, before your face is on a missing poster every five feet throughout all of Adhara."

Ryder and I exchange glances before he clamps a hand down on his brother's shoulders and guides him in the right direction.

He explains everything to him, with a few interruptions from Liam. He tells him about the journal, Barret and the sickness, why his soup was poisoned, and why that man tried to kill Liam.

"So Archer knows?" Liam interrupts what Ryder was saying.

"No, and don't interrupt me when I'm explaining something just to ask a question that would've been answered. King Archer didn't know about what was in the journal, he just knew that Dominant Point wanted to kill us to keep a secret. He didn't want to know what it was."

"Well, yeah, why would you go looking for the secret that makes the world leaders want you dead? Thanks for that, by the way. Being included in the gossip is *so* worth being told I can never go home. I would've worn softer clothes. These black *leather* pants would've been fine for an hour at most, but not-"

"*Stop. Talking.* In case you already forgot what I said *two minutes ago*, Dominant Point sent that guy to kill you because they assumed I would've already told you. You wouldn't have been able to go home now regardless of whether I kept you in the dark."

"Are you okay?" I interrupt their banter and both their eyes snap in my direction.

I grew up in the same palace as Liam, but I've never known him the way I know Ryder. But you don't have to know someone like the back of your hand to know they need someone to check on them after almost being murdered and being told that when they left home this morning they would never be going back.

"Oh yeah. Peachy." Liam says the last word as if it's the name of his greatest enemy. Ryder just rolls his eyes.

"Are you sure there's no way for you to ever safely communicate with anyone from home?" Liam's tone has lost the humor he usually carries with him. Ryder lets out an exasperated sigh.

"Yes. At least for now, it's not safe to attempt to communicate with anyone." Ryder keeps walking forward with the same unmoved expression until he notices Liam's scrunched brows and his teeth sinking into his lip, almost hard enough to draw blood.

"What?"

"Mom's gonna be devastated," Liam mumbles. Ryder's mask slips out of place at the mention of their mom.

"She was a wreck when they told her that no one knew where you were, and when they said that some of the food was missing, she just lost it. She thought that maybe she did something that made you wanna get away, or she didn't notice something else was wrong. I don't know. She just started listing every way she could blame herself for you running away," Liam says, looking up at the trees and away from us.

Ryder's breath stalls for a minute. I grab his hand and interlock our fingers. He squeezes and releases over and over again for the next few minutes.

"Maybe *eventually*, things will have settled down enough for you guys to try to get some kind of massage to your mom. Just to tell her you're safe and you love her," I suggest. Ryder shakes his head.

"Isa-"

"I'm not saying anytime soon. Probably not even within the next five years, but eventually." I try to look into his eyes, but he just keeps looking down.

"Look at you, all optimistic even though we're a group of three people that won't be able to bathe for a few days, after walking and sweating under the sun for hours," Liam says. *Ew.*

Ryder and Liam bicker back and forth for a bit while I try, as subtly as I can, to tilt my head at the right angle to smell myself. This, multiplied by the next few days, plus two boys...my optimism drains out nearly entirely.

"I'm just saying-" A blood curdling scream cuts off Liam's retort. The three of us exchange a quick look before taking off toward the sound.

As we get closer, the one loud scream fades into dozens of smaller screams and groans. We slow our pace, moving just far enough towards the edge of the trees to stay hidden from view.

The three of us crouch down, inching closer to the edge of a hill.

"Oh God." I don't even really feel the words come out of my mouth.

Below us, dozens and dozens of people lay in the streets, groaning and scratching at their skin. Some have blood draining from their eyes and ears, others lay so still you would think they're dead if it weren't for the whimpers.

There are a few people who don't seem to be in any physical pain. They just look either terrified or distraught. I don't-

I push my head into my hands and turn away. Bile works its way up my stomach. One of the people, who didn't look like she was in any physical pain, jammed a jagged rock into her neck, while a crying baby was strapped to her chest. Her blood spilled all over her wailing baby before her body collapsed on top of him.

I uncover my eyes and start to stand, only to be pulled back down.

"We have to help them!" I pull my arm out of Ryder's grasp. We could at least get the baby out from under her.

"The only thing you can do is get infected and end up just like them. Let's go." Ryder says.

My jaw drops. I whip my head around towards Liam, expecting to see some resistance to just leaving these people. The look on his face stirs something unpleasant in my chest. He looks back to the people, his brows pulled tightly together and his lip tucked between his teeth.

"Sorry, Isabelle, but Ryder's right. We can't do anything for them."

"But you had all that medical supplies. We can go back and tell them these people need help-"

"None of it was a cure. That stuff won't do anything to help these people." Liam's eyes look genuinely sympathetic as he avoids looking back at them. Ryder moves his hand from a firm grasp on mine to a gentle touch on my back.

"I'm sorry Isa, I know you want to help them, and I understand, but we need to go. We can't do anything for them."

"But-" His eyes shift from his typical calm mask to a pleading look.

"Okay." I agree.

That baby didn't even seem sick. I look back to his mothers body stacked on top of him and realize that his cries have stopped. His tiny, chubby fingers stick out from underneath her, entirely still.

I hear the sounds of pain from the sick as we walk away. It sears the images of them into my mind. It's horrific and painful, and seeing the sick and their loved ones crying over them makes me think I would rather be the one getting ripped to shreds by my own body than the one watching *this* happen to someone I care about.

It's the most horrific, ungodly, sickening thing I think could've ever existed, and it's not the sickness. It's the *people* who are making this happen.

The weight of our situation settles in at the reminder of why we left. We didn't leave to avoid getting sick. We left because the same people who would do this–this barbaric torture to a *baby* and anyone else for their own gain–are the same ones who want us dead.

CHAPTER 16

ISABELLE

Liam stopped taking every opportunity for humor, Ryder hasn't let go of my hand for even a second, and I haven't been able to stop thinking about the mother and baby in the hours that we've been walking without a break.

I haven't been able to shake this deep, sickening feeling. People are dying and they're going to keep dying so horribly, not even knowing that someone is doing this to them. The people who are supposed to protect us are killing mothers and their babies while being worshiped as the ones doing everything to help us.

I keep seeing that mother and her baby over and over again in my head. Did she regret it right after she slit open her neck? Did she realize her baby would die? Or was she in so much pain she couldn't even think about her baby? Did she watch over him as a ghost? Screaming and not being able to do anything to get her own body off of him?

And *how* can the people at Dominant Point watch this happen to innocent people and be happy about their plan? Not just happy, proud. In my mom's last entry, she said that Barret looked *proud* of his idea and the videos he was showing them.

That mother and baby, mothers watching their children die slowly and not dying until after their own children. People that want to live, or just want to keep the people they love safe. Everyone who only wants their family and themselves to be safe–and Barret just sits there, *proud of himself,* watching them all die.

We've been far away from the town for a while now, but I can still hear their screams echoing in my head. And I can still imagine the proud look my mother described on Barret's face as he showed Dominant Point videos of the people he killed.

The sun fully set maybe an hour ago, and none of us has said anything about when we're setting up camp for the night.

Even though we're out here because of a secret about the sickness, I had honestly pushed the actual sickness itself to the back of my mind. Just the three of us, isolated in a cabin for the rest of our lives, doesn't seem so bad any more.

At least then we won't ever come in contact with anyone who could get us sick. It feels insane to complain about that after seeing how much pain those people were in.

We walk through trees with no path in sight. With every step, we pull our knees up high to avoid tripping over all the roots and vines.

"Are you sure you're taking us the right way? Let me see that." Liam reaches for the map but Ryder yanks it away.

"Yes, I'm sure," Ryder says, staring his brother down in annoyance.

"This clearly isn't a path, it's the middle of the goddamn woods," Liam says.

"Why would we take a common path out in the open when we are wanted dead?" That shuts Liam up.

It's been dark out for a few hours now but we haven't wanted a break yet. I don't think any of us want to have the time to think about what happened back there.

The trees look mossy around the roots and the specks on the flower petals have an odd bit of glow, almost like the ones by the river next to the palace, but not as bright. The moss has a faint glow as well.

"Is there another glowing river over here?" I ask Ryder.

I notice him watching the glowing plants too before he answers me.

"Not that I know of. But the soil here seems damp. It's possible this whole area could have once been covered in water and now some of the algae is left behind in the damp soil."

"Pretty," Liam says as he plucks a flower and rolls the stem between his fingers.

As we keep walking the trees grow taller and denser, making it feel like a whole other world. Frogs croak all around us, and crickets chirp constantly.

It's a beautiful spot, most likely because very few people probably want to spend time in an area so dense with trees. The air even feels nice.

"Get down!" Liam whisper–shouts. Ryder and I immediately drop to the ground, looking around for the danger.

"Why? What do you see?" Ryder asks, his voice low and tense.

Liam points through a gap in the trees.

"There's a cabin over there. No one is supposed to see us."

I squint my eyes, peering through the trees until I see it. You can faintly see the roof of a cabin. It's close to us, but hidden.

Lowering my head, I inch forward on my hands and knees, getting a little bit closer until I see it at a new angle.

"I don't think anyone lives there, it looks old," I say. The cabin is mostly stone with a few chips off the corners of the walls. A few of the wooden pillars have completely eroded. Countless vines and weeds climb up the cabin, adding to how hidden it seems even when being so close.

"Isabelle's right," Ryder says, brushing off his pants as he stands up. "We'll check it out and if it seems clear that no one lives here, we'll stay for tonight then keep going in the morning."

"Thank God my first night on the run from the government won't be spent sleeping on the forest floor." Liam mutters, mostly to himself. He dusts off his pants and stands, stretching his arms as if he's already settling into the idea of a more comfortable night ahead.

As we get closer, I can tell that this place is incredibly old but was once very beautiful. Liam takes straight strides towards the front door before Ryder yanks him back by his shirt and motions us both to the window.

"Dude, obviously, no one lives here," Liam whispers, obviously frustrated by being yanked around like a wandering child. Ryder lets out an exasperated breath, looking like he's trying to refrain from strangling his brother. *This is why I hardly saw them spend time together in the palace.*

"This may not be anyone's home, but that doesn't mean there isn't someone spending the night in there if they have nowhere else to go." Ryder says quietly. We all move slowly towards the window and peer inside. It's covered in thick layers of dust. I doubt anyone has been here in years.

"It should be safe, we'll check each window around the house just to be sure, then go inside." Ryder gestures for us to keep moving around the side of the moss covered cabin.

"Yes sir, your Highness." Liam mocks, even though he was the one destined to be king of Adhara. Around the back of the cabin, there are stone dividers and tiny walls that might've once served as divisions in a garden.

"I would guess that was the last person to live here," Liam says, pointing to a stone a few feet away.

I move away from the side of the house to get a better look. It's a headstone with words carved into it. The rock is eroded, every carving has been softened but it can still faintly be made out.

It says 'My Brutal Love' with a squiggle below it that might have once been a flower. The ground surrounding it is covered in Night's Petal flowers but they especially group together over the grave. Whoever buried their 'Brutal Love' must've covered the grave in these flowers and they spread all over the place.

"There's no one here," Liam says as he and Ryder come back from around the house. "You guys can keep staring at that grave, but I'm going to bed. Also if there's only one bed, I call dibs." Liam yanks open the rusted door as Ryder and I follow him inside.

"No, Isabelle and I have been out the longest, so we deserve the bed." The two of them bicker back and forth as I take in the space around us. The kitchen and living room are pushed into one open room and everything in here looks very, very old.

There are only two other doors. One is open and revealing a bathroom that, with the style of its toilet and sink, makes it look like this place may be centuries old. I assume the other door leads to a bedroom. Liam stands in front of the bedroom door with his arms crossed.

"Someone tried to kill me today, I deserve the bed."

"Get over it, someone tried to kill me two days ago."

"It's fine," I cut in, "Ryder and I can take the living room."

"Are you sure? Those couches look...old." Ryder's lip curls in disgust as he eyes the two musty couches.

"She's sure!" Liam yells as he slams the bedroom door behind himself.

"The windows are broken so with all the Night's Petals out there it smells nice in here." I point out. Ryder moves his head back and forth, considering.

"Okay then." He walks over to the center table between the two couches that face each other and carefully lifts the lid to pull out a few blankets. He sorts through them. They all look a little stiff, they've probably sat in that table for the last twenty decades, maybe more.

He lays a few out over one couch and a few out over the other, then takes a very hesitant seat. As soon as my butt touches the couch across from him, Liam comes out of his room dragging a skeleton by the feet.

He swings open the back door and chucks out the skeleton. Liam brushes his hands off with his lip curled in a disgusted look.

"I found Brutal Love's lover. Ew, God, gross." He gags then walks back into his room.

That was...odd.

I look over to Ryder, an exhausted look pulls on his face.

"He's driven you crazy that quickly?" I ask. He smiles a sad, weary smile and shakes his head. "Are you okay?" Guilt creeps back into me for being the one to put him in this position.

"I don't know." He buries his face in his hands, elbows propped on his knees. God, he looks so miserable.

"I'm sorry," I whisper. My chin wobbles at the sight of him, knowing he's sitting here because of me. Even if he says he isn't mad at me, it's still my fault. His lack of anger or blame doesn't change that. He shakes his head while keeping it propped in his hands.

"It's not your fault. You don't–"

"You're both here because of what I showed you, that's my fault. He was going to be *king,* and you had so much ahead of you and you–Oh, your poor mom. I took both her sons away from her, and she doesn't even know why you're gone or if you're okay, and she won't see you again and she didn't get to say goodbye because of me–" Tears build up in my eyes and my throat tightens.

I love their mom. She used to do my hair for me after my mom left. She did all these little things I would've only expected from my mother. There were so many times I sat in her lap and cried about missing my mom while I squeezed her tight. She always held me, telling me she loved me.

She's the reason life wasn't as bad as it could've been after my mom left, and now she must be in so much pain because of what I did.

"Isabelle, you didn't do anything wrong. There is a difference between your actions leading to something bad and doing a bad thing. If a child sneezed so somebody looked over, and that caused them to trip which made them fall on a butterfly, you wouldn't say that child killed a butterfly. You are not a bad person, please don't talk about yourself like you are." He lifts his head from his hands to look at me. My stomach pinches as I take in the tears filling his eyes.

"That's not what it feels like right now," I mumble, not wanting to speak too loudly so he doesn't hear the shake in my voice. His brows pull together and up in a sympathetic look.

"You–Do you think I'm a bad person?" he asks. My head tilts to the side.

"No? Of course not." He's the furthest thing in the world from a bad person. When we were little he would kiss my scraped knees, and when I missed my mom he would always make me laugh, even if it meant embarrassing himself.

"I used to watch my father beat Liam while he begged me to help him, and I did nothing," he says, looking me in the eyes with a flat expression. "Our father thought the way he behaved was improper and that's how he chose to deal with it. Truthfully, I guess it's part of the reason I get so annoyed by Liam. Every stupid, badly timed, unfunny excuse for a joke is proof that he's stronger than me. Liam never stopped being himself. I followed my father's every instruction and constantly thought of what he would tell me to do before he could even say it. That's why I never helped Liam. I still ended up with more scars than him anyway. Every cruelty my father did, I always stood by his side. I thought like a soldier.

"I wasn't upset because of anything you caused. I was upset because I know the only reason I've been able to keep a level head is because of the lessons he taught me. I *hate* that anything he's given could actually help me. I hate reminding myself of him so much in any high stress environment. He's a monster, and I could handle the sick feeling of being like him when he's around and I know why I'm doing it. But to revert to that person now, when he's not here, I hate it.

"I only ever felt like myself when I was with you in the palace. Everywhere else, I had to be who I had to be. But with you, it's safe. I'm happiest when I'm with you. It may be the only time I'm truly happy. I know it's the only time I'm happy with myself. So I swear I'm not mad at you for us being here, even if it were your fault. I'm *excited* to live the rest of my life with my best friend. I am so much more excited for this life than for anything I could've had as a royal. I may not deserve it, but I want this. Spending the rest of my days with my best friend sounds amazing." I choke out a small laugh, wiping the tears that fell from my eyes.

"And Liam." I say.

"Him too."

I stand up to hug him but stop straight in the middle of the two couches. Ryder looks up at me with a new look on his face, he heard it too. The floor beneath my feet is creaky and hollow. Hesitantly, I pick up my foot and stomp. An echo rings out from beneath us.

Ryder stands and slides the center table to the side, then lifts the old, color–faded rug, revealing a hatch.

He looks up at me, not yet touching the handle to pull the door open. I crouch down beside him and pull the door open myself, the smell of salt immediately floods my nostrils.

There are rickety looking wooden steps leading all the way down, which looks like a short distance. A few of the steps are completely broken.

Ryder inches forward, testing his weight on the first step before slowly making his way down to the hidden lower level. I swing my legs in front of me from my crouched position and follow after him. My butt hovers a few inches above the steps and my hands grip the steps behind me, bracing myself in case the steps collapse. I look up from the rickety steps beneath me, finally getting a clear view of the new level.

The walls are made of sand and salt solidified into stone, curving into the ceiling in an oval shape. The whole level looks like it could stretch on for maybe a hundred feet.

Tiny strings of light filter in from the ceiling, starting beyond where the cabin ends. But most of the light doesn't come from the holes in the ceiling.

Most of the level is just water. The water here glows much brighter than the river. It's a glowing, luminous, crystal blue color fading into pale sand ground, walls, and ceiling.

There's about twenty or so feet of hilly, bumpy ground in front of Ryder and me before it fades into water. Ryder sits on one of the largest ridges next to us, then folds his legs in front of himself.

This hidden level feels like a whole other world than the one just a few feet above us. I take a seat next to Ryder on the solid sand ridge and lean my head against his shoulder.

In this moment, it doesn't feel like anything bad could be waiting for us above this place.

There's only us, the pale sand, and the glowing water.

He grabs my hand, interlaces his fingers with mine, and neither of us says a word.

CHAPTER 17

ISABELLE

My eyes snap open at the sound of the back door slamming shut. The algae outside, paired with the moon and starlight shining in is enough for me to see fairly well.

Ryder is sleeping on the couch across from me, wrapped up in a knitted blanket that's falling apart, and there aren't any swarms of assassins sent by Dominant Point—at least not yet. Unless they're hiding behind the couch, ready to cut my head off.

I slowly sit up on the couch, still keeping my head low. It really doesn't look like anyone's here and it's a fairly open layout so there aren't many places to hide. Although I'm sure anyone sent by Dominant Point would be able to figure something out.

The floor creaks beneath my weight as I step off the couch, bracing myself to be tackled by someone hiding in the shadows. I check behind both couches, scan the open room again, then make my way towards the bedroom to make sure no one is strangling Liam.

I don't know why they would walk straight past us and go into another room where Liam may or may not be, but it's better to be safe than burying Liam.

Before I can turn towards his room something catches my eye. Liam's sitting out back on the porch steps. He must've been the one who woke me up by shutting the door.

A half shiver, half yawn rolls through me as I step towards the door. I have no idea what time it is, but the sky doesn't look any closer to sunrise than it did when we got here. Thank God. I could easily sleep another eighteen hours right now.

Liam jolts as I pull the creaking door open. Looking back at Ryder to make sure I didn't wake him, I guide the door shut as quietly as possible.

"Hey, how are you doing?" I ask, settling down beside him. Whoever lived here was very lucky, this place is beautiful at night. The flowers glow so beautifully and the white ones look almost magical.

Glowing moss climbs up the trees, fruit and berries grow all over the yard, likely overgrown from the original garden area. It looks like something straight out of a fairy tale.

"You know, same old, same old. Not much to report," he says, waving his hand carelessly through the air.

"What are you doing out here?" I ask.

"Couldn't sleep. Maybe the ghost of that skeleton is pissed I threw him, so he's haunting me." Liam mumbles.

"Mmh, makes sense." I hesitate, debating whether or not I should just go back inside. I would like to help him or at least let him talk about what he's feeling, but we aren't very close.

It would make sense if he isn't interested in opening up to me and just wants to be left alone for a little while. This is also just kind of awkward.

"Are you excited to spend the rest of your life with two spoiled boys in one cabin and no socialization with anyone else in the world?" he asks, with an almost painfully fake smile.

"You mean, am I excited to watch two spoiled boys live without servants and palace luxuries for the first time? I can't wait."

He laughs a shallow, humorless laugh. "Fair enough."

"And how are you feeling about it?" I ask again. He may just not be the kind of person who wants to talk about his feelings. Which would be a shame, because I'm awful at comforting people so I typically just ask how they're doing then nod my head.

"I feel like I just lost everything. I mean, I *did*, right? I'm never going to see my mom again, never going to sleep in my bed, and I'm never going to see any of my friends. I'll never get back what I had. Everything I was looking forward to is gone. I was actually *excited* about being king. I know a lot of other crowned royals are nervous about having so much responsibility, but to me it felt like it wouldn't be as much pressure or responsibility as going to Dominant Point.

"Adhara is such a big kingdom. I could've made sure children get a better education and families never, ever go hungry. I was going to cut how much taxes were spent on royal luxuries we don't even need, and instead have the majority of taxes spent on actually improving the lives of my people. Everything I spent every day of my life thinking about is gone."

Wow. I'd never heard him talk about his plans for the kingdom or how much it meant to him. I had honestly just assumed he didn't understand or appreciate the kind of power and opportunity he had right at his fingertips.

I put my hand over his as we admire the view, silence stretching between us.

"I'm sorry," I say.

"It's okay, it's not your fault."

Ryder told him that we found out about the sickness from *my* mom's journal. I wonder if part of him blames me for everything he's feeling right now. If he does, he isn't showing it.

"Just because you won't have the life you expected, it doesn't mean your life is over. Maybe you'll develop a passion for bird watching or gardening. Maybe we'll find a stray dog to become your best friend, or the cabin will be filled with hundreds of books for you to spend your life reading. I know it won't be the life you imagined, but there could still be something good made from it."

Maybe we can celebrate the day we get to the cabin as a holiday. When we used to celebrate the joining of Dominant Point, the servants would wait until the royals went to bed before celebrating.

We would stay up all night eating soup, bread, and roasted chicken. To finish it off, five servants would have a contest for the best dessert. Everyone was happy, laughing, with bellies full of food and people who, for a night, felt like family.

The three of us could come up with some traditions and create our own holiday, something to make life a little more bearable.

"Such an optimist." he says, wrapping an arm around my shoulder. "In case you were wondering, I don't blame you for this, by the way. It's not your fault your mom was eavesdropping on the wrong conversation, and it's not your fault my uncle is a homicidal maniac. Shit just happens."

He shakes me by the shoulder once then lets go. "And you're right. It's gonna suck compared to being a prince waiting to be king, but we'll be alive, and I'm an absolute delight to have around. You guys really lucked out by having me tag along, you're welcome."

"Yeah, thank goodness your uncle sent someone to kill you, or we would be so bored." He shoves me and laughs just a little, though this one doesn't sound entirely miserable.

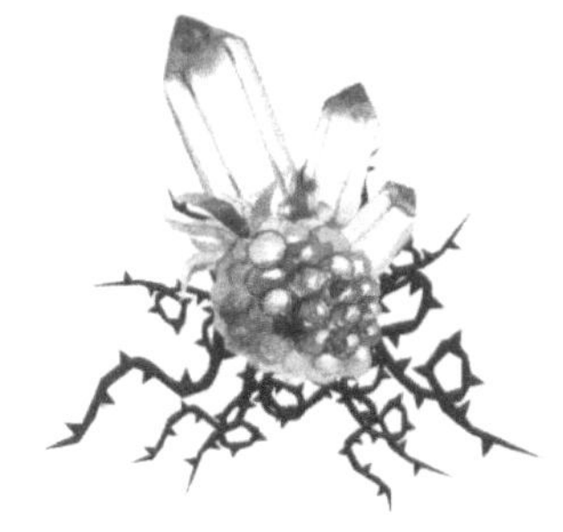

CHAPTER 18

ISABELLE

I woke up to Ryder and Liam bickering. Liam was groaning for just one more hour of sleep, while Ryder was saying he doesn't care if we have to leave him there. Eventually, Liam dragged himself out of the bed he'd found a skeleton on and yet still slept like a baby in.

At least while we were there I was able to change out of the nightgown Archer woke me up in and put on my uniform. It's ugly and scratchy, but it was either this or my going into town dress. If I end up having to run for my life, I think pants would be better.

We got to have some of the berries growing all over the cabin's backyard before we left, which was nice, but right now we don't need berries. We need meat and bread.

We've been walking towards King Archer's uncle's cabin all day now. A few short breaks helped, but they didn't do much to recharge us given our low rations.

Ryder and I had packed a decent amount for the two of us, but we hadn't planned for an extra mouth to feed. Now, we don't have enough to make it through the last day of our walk. We'll survive one day without food, but paired with walking all day under the sun, we'll be miserable.

Ryder tried to give me some of his rations each time we took a break but I refused. Mostly because I can't make out the landmarks he drew on the map and neither can Liam. So, he needs to eat at least enough to think clearly and follow the landmarks he drew on the map. Ryder's extraordinarily talented at many things, but art definitely isn't one of them.

All of us are hungry and a little cranky. Liam and Ryder have been taking it out on each other for the past six hours of useless bickering and now they're both just ignoring each other.

Finally.

"Look!" Liam whisper–shouts while pointing through the trees.

"Wow, a deer in a forest." Ryder deadpans.

I look through the trees at where Liam is pointing. There's a very pretty deer eating grass, completely unaware we're watching. It's cute and has lashes like a children's book drawing, but it's not exactly a big deal. Deer are common in these woods.

"No idiot, I mean we could hunt it. We need food, and not just flowers." Liam looks back at me.

I ate a few flowers earlier, which are all completely edible and have lots of health benefits. They're just not very filling. Their loss though, I'm slightly less hungry than they are.

"Hunt it with what? Do you plan on throwing rocks at it?" Ryder asks.

"Hunting's not a bad idea though. We could set up some kind of trap," I say. Liam's right, we need real food, and Ryder's right that we can't kill a deer.

Also, I don't really want to. None of us are skilled enough with long range weapons to give her a painless death.

"Using a trap is a good idea. What did you have in mind?" Ryder asks.

"Good idea, **Isabelle,** *you're so smart. Liam would never think of hunting an animal.* Oh wait! He did*."* Liam mocks.

"Her idea wasn't to kill a deer with no weapons." Ryder snaps back.

I interrupt them, "Well, we've seen a lot of bunnies in this area. We could dig a hole, cover it with a few leaves, then place any berries we could find around it." It kills me a little to say it. I had a pet bunny named Paws for about a week when I was little but my mom made me let him go.

"That's good. Liam, you go find some berries, Isabelle and I will dig a hole," Ryder instructs.

"Um in case you forgot I was going to be *king,* not some errand boy."

"And I was going to be your superior, but instead, we're here and hungry. Please just get some berries so we can set up a trap and have enough food to last us until we get to the cabin."

I've never seen Ryder be hangry. Although, I also don't think he's ever been hungry in his life until now and I've never seen him be angry in any way. He usually just walks away from Liam after a few seconds so this doesn't happen.

"There's bunny poop right over there. We could dig the trap here," I suggest.

"Okay. Liam, come back here with whatever you've found in one hour." Ryder says, then motions for his brother to leave.

"Yeah, because I'm carrying a clock with me and I'll know exactly when it's been an hour." Liam mumbles as he walks away.

Ryder picks up a stick and starts tracing a circle in the dirt while I dig through our bag for whatever rations we have left. We've already eaten all the meat, so now we're down to nuts and dried fruit.

"Here," I say, holding out a small bag of nuts. He pushes my hand back.

"No, it's okay. I'll wait until we catch something. You go ahead." I stuff the nuts back into the bag instead. "You can still eat some now, you've barely eaten enough." I don't think he saw just how many flowers I ate, which is probably a good thing.

"I'll wait too."

He uses his stick to loosen the dirt within the circle he drew. I start to grab my own stick to help but before I can pick one up he tosses his stick aside and begins scooping up the loosened dirt with his hands.

I help him scoop dirt until my arms feel like jelly, my nails are caked in dirt, and we've dug a narrow hole deep enough that a bunny shouldn't be able to jump out.

"Liam should be coming back now, assuming he's not lost," Ryder says. Liam may not be the best at reading the room, but I don't think he's actually stupid. He should be able to find his way back here.

The sound of footsteps crushing twigs and leaves gradually grows louder in the distance.

Ryder and I sit by our hole, waiting for Liam to get back so we can set up our trap and eat real, filling food. I watch Ryder sitting across from me. He doesn't look like he's doing well. His face is completely neutral, but it's his body language that shows he's still feeling just as uneasy as he was when we talked last night.

He looks sick too, or malnourished. The sun has tanned his skin into a little bit of a healthy glow, but his cheeks are sunken and his muscles have started depleting.

He looks tortured.

It reminds me of how he looks in his royal portrait from his sixteenth birthday. He looked beautiful, he usually does. All anyone ever said about it were compliments on his beautiful green eyes and soft brown hair. People have talked about how pretty he is for as long as I can remember.

But in that painting, he looked more sick than attractive. His dad had been pressuring him about how important the portrait was, growing sterner the closer his birthday came. By the time he was getting the portrait done, he hadn't been able to keep any food down for days due to the stress and his father had beaten him or yelled at him for every tiny thing at least twice a day. But all anyone saw was green eyes, dark brown hair, and sharp bone structure.

He looks eerily similar to that painting now.

His brows pull together and his hand snaps up. I pull myself out of my thoughts and listen for what might have caught his attention. The footsteps are constant, not like just one person moving one foot at a time. He looks back and forth, listening intently. Ryder shoots up to his feet, grabs my arm, and pulls us both behind a tree surrounded by bushes.

"There's a group of people." Ryder whispers in my ear.

The sounds of snapping twigs and crunching leaves grows closer until whoever they are, they're right behind our tree. It could always just be a group of people going on a walk, it is a nice day out. I slowly turn to look behind the tree, careful not to disturb a single branch or blade of grass.

It's five people, all dressed in head to toe black uniforms and armed heavily.

"Remember, if you see the servant aim for one in the head, if you see the princes shoot to maim, not kill."

Ryder wraps his arms around my waist and pulls me back behind the tree. I scootch into him a little bit more in an attempt to shrink us.

"Andrew was found dead at the location we sent him to find Liam not too far from here. They're close, and they'll kill you if they get the chance. Do not hesitate to fire." The same man orders.

He must be in charge of them, but he's not a part of Dominant Point. I've met, or at least seen, all of them. He just works for them.

"Why are we now shooting to maim?" Another one asks.

"Orders change, it's not our place to question it. Barret's instructions for the servant remain the same, if you see her, kill her."

Ryder pulls me in closer, holds his hand holding the back of my head. My ear is pressed against his chest, I can feel his rapid heart beat thumping furiously. He's afraid.

A few leaves brush together further down the hill on our side of the tree. I move my head away from Ryder and glance over. Liam's walking towards us, swatting at every branch that gets in his way, completely unaware of the people waiting to shoot him as soon as they hear him.

If we move, they'll either see us or hear us moving in the bushes. And if he gets any closer, they'll see him and find all of us.

Liam finally looks up from the berries he's been tossing back and forth in his hands and sees us crouched down together.

He gives us both a confused look, then makes the face he always does right before he says something stupid or complains about what we're doing.

Ryder frantically signals for him to get down. It could either look like he's telling him to get down or motioning for him to come here. He's just pointing down.

"What?"

"Shut the fuck up," I see Ryder silently mouth out. Liam's face drops, maybe he caught a glimpse of the people on the other side of the tree. He immediately drops down. The sound of dirt and sand falling beneath his weight travels clearly all the way here. I hold my breath and squeeze in every part of myself. If they look over here and see even the slightest hint of my elbow sticking out, I'm dead, and God knows what will happen to Liam and Ryder.

"Did you guys hear that?" one of them asks.

Ryder pulls me in closer and moves so that I'm in between him and the tree. The men move closer to us. I clamp my hand over my mouth, trying as hard as I can to stifle my rapid breathing.

I tighten my arms around Ryder as they step closer and closer. Spending the rest of my life in that cabin doesn't sound bad at all now. I don't want to be here. I want to go home. I want to lay in a bed, in a safe place, wrapped in a blanket. I want to see my mom again. I want to hug Ryder just to hug him, and not because I may die.

I shift my head a tiny bit away from Ryder to peek out. They're here. The man who seems to be in charge is standing two feet away from me, looking out at the down hill area beneath us.

I hold in a sob until my entire body is shaking. If a grasshopper chirps next to us or a butterfly lands on a flower by my feet and it catches his attention, the man I'm looking at, the man who's right above me and doesn't even know it, will put a bullet in my brain. Right now. Without a second thought.

"This way," the man motions for his team to follow him. I watch all five of them walk past me and Ryder, waiting for one of them to see us. They move down the hill with guns in their hands, but luckily, they're not heading directly towards Liam.

They're about ten or so feet away from where Liam dropped to the ground. Depending on how well he's hidden that might just barely be enough. The leader was two feet away from us and he didn't notice. Liam could be fine.

They get further and further down the hill to where Liam was. With all the bushes and trees around, he should've been able to hide well. I hold Ryder's hand, squeezing it tighter the closer they get to Liam. They're exactly as far away from us as Liam is, just a little to the left. They look around for a moment, then continue walking.

Ryder and I both relax. I drop my arms back to my side and finally breathe steady. As long as they keep walking and don't turn around, we'll be okay.

One by one, they each disappear. I move up to get a better look at what happened but Ryder pulls me back down. There's a small ditch down there, that must be where Liam hid.

Each of the men climb back out the other side and continue walking. If Liam is down there, he hid well enough to avoid being seen by others in the ditch.

Ryder holds me tightly as we watch the men walk away, slowly disappearing behind the trees. We listen for the sound of their foot falls, waiting for them to fade completely.

Once the noise dies down enough to assume they're a safe distance away, Ryder stands up, grabs my hand, and runs towards the ditch Liam is hiding in.

We race down the hill. Urgency pulses through my veins, screaming at me to run faster. When we reach the ditch, Ryder lets go of my hand for me to slide down first.

If they were to come back right now, they would see me instantly, and I would be dead before I even knew they were here.

I slide down the dirt and rocks on my butt, my heart pounding in my chest. Ryder follows behind me, using his hands and feet to carefully descend the steep, rubble wall. The ditch is mostly dirt and sand, with vines and branches spilling over the walls from the plants above.

"Liam? Liam?" Ryder whisper–shouts, his voice tight with urgency.

"Over here," I turn around to follow the muffled reply. Liam's voice is barely audible, hidden behind a thick collection of vines and leaves hanging over the wall of the ditch.

Ryder and I quickly squeeze in beside him, pulling the vines back into place as our thin cover.

"Dominant Point?" Liam asks, his voice strained and breathless.

Ryder and I exchange a glance then nod.

"We'll stay here until we're sure they won't come back this way." Ryder says. It's going to be hours before we can be sure they've gone off to look somewhere else. But right now, staying hidden behind plants with bugs and spiders crawling through and creeping over our skin, pressed against the cold damp earth, feels like the safest place we've had since we left the palace.

I squeeze my eyes shut and hold my knees to my chest. Ryder, Liam, and I stay huddled together for hours, and I keep my eyes shut with my head between my knees the whole time.

It's completely silent until it begins to rain. The soft sound of droplets hitting the ground grows harder and harder for about an hour as a reminder that there is still a world outside of these vines.

"Isabelle," Ryder rests his hand on my back, "We can get out now. It should be safe." He says gently. None of us have said a word for hours. Liam pushes the vines to the side, and we all stand to brush ourselves off.

The dirt we were sitting on turned to mud a while ago, and the rain dripping off the vines soaked us completely. My hunger doesn't even feel like hunger anymore. It feels more like a deep, full body weakness.

I drag my feet up the hill. Nausea and heat roll over me in painful waves. Once we've reached the top, I drop to my knees and crawl over to the hole we'd dug. We didn't have any bait, so it's a long shot but maybe, just maybe...

Relief floods over me when I see a small black rabbit struggling to escape the hole.

"Thank God," Liam breaths when he looks over my shoulder at the rabbit.

It's very cute, and very scared.

I reach down to pick it up. He fights and wiggles against my grasp at first, but calms down a little when I cradle him to my chest.

"It's okay, baby. You're okay," I whisper, softly running my fingers over his forehead and slowly down his fluffy, curved back.

I wonder if this is at all soothing for him. Maybe he knows I don't *want* to hurt him, that I don't want him to feel the way I felt when I was hiding and looking at the man ready to kill me, or maybe he just knows he's in the arms of his predator.

I glance up at Liam and nod. He reaches down as I continue to pet the bunny. The bunny fights and kicks as hard as he can to escape the moment Liam's hand meets the bunny's neck, all the way until a quick and hard twist of Liam's wrist.

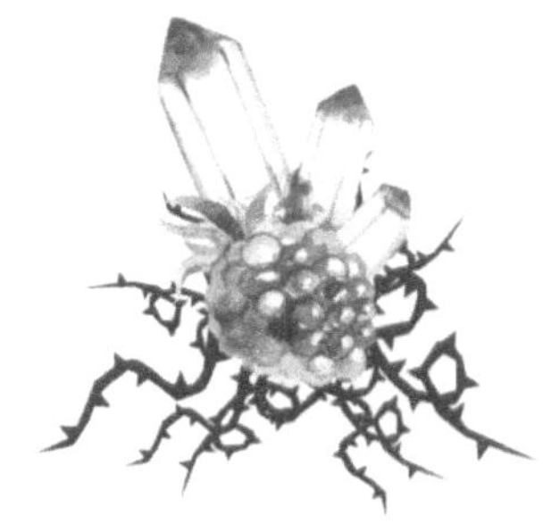

Chapter 19

Isabelle

If I focus more on my surroundings than on my depleting energy, it's not too bad.

We kept walking for a couple more hours after we ate and now I feel like I'm dead. Eating helped, I'm not hungry any more, but the adrenaline rise and crash drained every bit of energy out of me.

The sun has started setting and the air is finally getting cooler. I take a deep breath in through my nose and try to focus on the smells around me–flowers, grass, and fresh air. We only have a couple more days until we reach the cabin. If we're smart, we'll be okay.

Those guys were right on top of us and didn't even notice. We'll keep preserving rations. We'll keep hunting. We'll keep walking. And we won't forget that Dominant Point is still out there, still looking.

The birds have started chirping their bedtime song to each other, and the ribbits of frogs grow louder with every passing minute. The field we're walking through now is fairly open, with tall grass and yellow flowers stretching all the way up the hill.

Ryder nudges us in a new direction, me more gently than Liam. He leads us off our path without a word and into the trees.

"That spot over there looks like a good place to settle down for the night. We'll keep going as soon as the sun comes up tomorrow. Is that okay, Isabelle?" Ryder says, pointing to a small patch of ground that's relatively smooth, tucked away in a ring of dense trees.

"This place is good." I agree.

To my own disappointment, Liam doesn't make some kind of remark about his brother not asking what he thinks. His comments can be annoying at the wrong moments but that's never stopped him before.

We're all still shell shocked and tired, but Liam's usually the last one to tap out of a good mood. I was hoping he would cheer us up just a little, or at least annoy us.

We don't say much as Ryder and I pull out our blankets and lay them down on the grass.

"I want you guys to know it really sucks being the only one who wasn't told they would be spending days walking through the kingdom."

A small smile tugs at my lips at his mild complaining. He's curled up on his side in a fetal position, knees to his chest, arms crossed, lying right on the slightly damp grass. It's an awkward pose for a fairly buff guy.

I scootch off my blanket and fold it in my arms just to drop it on top of him. He opens one eye in a skeptical look before smirking.

"Thank you. You show me more kindness than my own flesh and blood." He wiggles his shoulders to snuggle against the blanket.

"That's her blanket, not yours. Give it back." Ryder says. Liam bolts upright.

"She gave it to me!"

"I don't care-"

"Can't I just share your blanket?" I ask Ryder. I honestly hadn't planned on being a saint and having no blanket all night. We have sleepovers all the time in the palace.

"Of course," he shifts to one side of his blanket and smooths the empty side, flattening out the wrinkles and tapping different parts of it like he might be fluffing a pillow.

I tuck myself into his side over the blanket that's clearly only meant for one person. Liam watches us with one brow raised before shaking it off, probably realizing he doesn't care, then shuts his eyes.

Now that I think about it, he probably doesn't know Ryder and I have been sharing a bed for years. To be fair, no one is supposed to know.

At some point in the night, after twisting and turning against Ryder and feeling goosebumps all over my skin, Ryder untangles his arms from mine, moves off the blanket, and tucks his half on top of me. I was so sleepy I couldn't really tell if it was real or not.

I look over my shoulder, expecting to see Ryder laying against a tree, but no one's there.

It's still pitch black, except for the stars and moonlight casting a faint glow dimmed even more by the trees. My eyes adjust slowly, shapes barely forming in the shadows.

"Ryder? Liam?" I sit up, half the blanket pools around my waist. It's chilly. It's dark. And the more it sinks in that I have no idea where they are, the more suffocating the worry becomes. More for them than myself.

I hang my head between my shoulders for a moment, trying to shake off the fog of sleep, urging myself to just fully wake up already.

All it takes is the snap of a twig in the distance to have me alert.

Anything could be out there and a dozen things could hurt or kill me right now: the government, a wild animal, flesh eating bugs–

No. Ew. Stop thinking about that.

Of everything out there, the one thing that matters most is that Liam and Ryder *aren't here.*

My eyes have adapted just enough for me to be sure that Liam's blanket is definitely empty and so is the space next to me.

"Ryder?" I push the blanket off and get to my feet, squinting through the trees. "Liam? Where are you? Guys? Hello?"

Please come back.

A rustling sound behind me nearly makes me jump out of my skin.

"Isabelle, Run!"

"Ryder?"

Before I can turn towards his voice, or even take a second to process his command, something hits me in the head, *hard.*

My body slams down to the ground, my vision swirling around the sky and tips of trees. I can faintly hear Ryder yelling something at somebody. Some type of commotion or fight, I don't know, I'm not even sure if I know how to stand. The sound seems almost like it's muffled by cotton, or coming from the other side of a door.

Someone climbs on top of me, pinning me down. I don't know why this person bothers. It's not like I was about to stand up and sprint through the forest. I can barely even attempt to pull my legs or arms up.

"What are you-" My words feel fuzzy coming out of my mouth, I'm not even sure I really said them.

Before I can finish my maybe unsaid words something sharp pricks the side of my neck. The dizzy fogginess becomes all encompassing until there's just nothing.

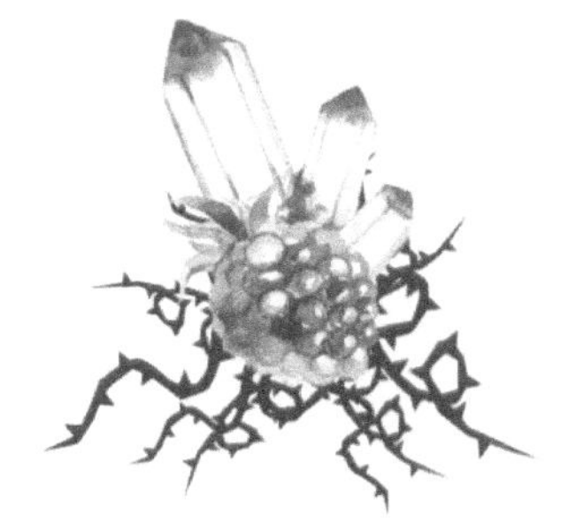

CHAPTER 20

This blanket is way stiffer than anything Ryder would've packed. I doubt any fabric this uncomfortable has ever even touched his skin.

It's surprisingly cold for this time of year. The light shining through my eyelids is bright enough that it must be day time already. I should feel the sun against my skin, but I don't.

My eyes flutter open like weights are tied to my eyelashes.

Definitely not outside, definitely not Ryder's blanket.

Right as I try to take in my surroundings, my heart jumps up to my throat. I scramble to the back of the bed as quickly as possible, but it only gives me a few more inches.

There's a man sitting at the end of it, perched in a fragile looking chair with his elbows resting on his knees.

I've never seen him before in my life.

The events of last night come rushing back to me. I may have never *seen* him, but I'm guessing I met him last night.

"Don't be afraid," he holds out a hand. His eyes are kind and sympathetic. Still, I edge back even farther until I'm centimeters from falling to the ground.

"What-Who-who are you?"

"My name's Kaito. I'm not going to hurt you, you can relax." I don't, at all. He gives me a small, half smile "That's understandable."

I look him up and down. He's tall even in his crouched position, not exactly buff, but far from skinny or fat. If he wanted to hurt me he definitely could.

His name while taking in his physical appearance finally jogs something in my memory.

"Are you from Cassiopeia?" I ask.

It's not possible.

Kaito Cassiopiea was the prince meant to be sent to Dominant Point but he died before he could, many years ago. It was big news at the time. Any royal death is, but it was shortly after my mom left, so I couldn't bring myself to really care.

"Yes, I am. I'll explain that to you soon but there are other matters I think would interest you more."

His hair and eyes are nearly black. He has the same face shape I vaguely remember seeing in a painting. Most importantly, he has a heart shaped birthmark on his left hand. He's many years older than the last remaining pictures of him before his 'death', but it's him.

That's the deceased Kaito Cassiopiea sitting in front of me. Breathing.

"Where are my friends?" The muscles in my shoulders slowly start to relax. My body gradually adapts to the thought that I may not be in imminent danger, at least not this minute.

He nods his head and quickly licks his lips.

"Liam was the first to wake up, about three hours ago. He was hesitant at first, much like you, but he calmed down. He's been out of his room for the last two hours. Last I saw him he was laughing with a group of young women and enjoying a slice of cake. Speaking of which, would you like me to have a slice saved for you? If there's any left? I'll admit, most of our food is for survival not enjoyment, so when we do have something like this, it's gone fairly quickly."

"What about Ryder?" The kindly smile vanishes from his face, replaced by something more measured, carefully neutral and practiced. Political. Once a royal, always a royal.

"We had to sedate him again."

"*What?*" My body tenses back up, this time with anger, not fear.

"When he woke up he was less willing to listen. He got agitated when we told him you were still asleep. When we said we didn't want him to see you until you woke up, and wanted him to first listen to what we had to say, he started to get hostile. So we sedated him."

His tone is smooth and calm, like he expects that to make me relax when he says my friend is sedated and in the hands of strangers.

"Why wouldn't you just let him see me while I was still asleep? Or wake me up?"

"I thought it would be best if you each had time for me to explain why you're here. To calm down before meeting with each other."

I gape at him. This 'everything is okay and you're the one being irrational' tone is getting on my nerves.

"So why *are* we here? And why are you alive? Why does everyone think you're dead?"

"I-"

"How long will Ryder be asleep?"

"Ms. Blum, please don't ask me questions if you won't let me answer them." Being called by my last name makes me cringe. I feel about twelve years older than I am.

"How do you know my name? Did Liam tell you?"

Liam does seem like he would mention my name in passing once he's calmed down. Especially knowing he has cake and women laughing at his jokes right now.

"No, he actually refused to tell me anything about you two. I didn't ask him to, but as soon as he woke up, he sternly said he 'wasn't talking'."

He gives a small laugh.

"I already know what I need to know about the three of you. I would like to get to know you more with your stay here, but as far as necessity, I believe I know enough."

"Our stay? How long do you plan on keeping us?" My body flips between relaxed and tense so often, I feel like I might get whiplash.

"I apologize, I should have phrased that differently. You are not captives here. We brought you here to help you."

"Who's we?"

"Everyone else at The Haven. That's what we call this place. Are you ready for me to explain or would you like a few more minutes to continue asking questions one after the other?" Despite his annoyance at my earlier interruptions, he seems patient. Most importantly, I believe him that my friends and I aren't in danger, for now.

"Explain." I stiffen up, no longer hanging off the side of my bed.

"Actually most of this goes back to your mother. She–"

"*My mother?*"

Do you know where she is? Do you know if she's okay? Is she *here?* Is that why I was brought here? She wanted to see me again?

Tears imminently fill my eyes at the thought that after all this time, she may have been looking after me and was able to bring me here.

Maybe *she* sent the anonymous letter. I'm going to get to hug her again! I'm gonna get to fall asleep next to her. I'm going to-

"Yes, your mother. And I'll allow that interruption but I would greatly prefer if you wouldn't say anything until I'm done. It will make this much easier." He looks at me with slightly widened eyes, telling me to shut up, politely.

I just nod, quickly. I'm ready to get to the end of this. I don't care anymore about anything he's saying. I just wanna see my mom again. I can almost feel my arms wrapping around her loving, soft, mom body. I can almost smell the rose scent of her hair.

"I knew your mother back when you were just a baby. She was a single mom, and I knew her through a friend of a friend. I saw how hard she was working to raise you so I would often help out. I was stationed at Dominant Point for training in the outer group, and her place in Polaris wasn't far from Dominant Point. I would come over some nights to cook dinner or clean up while she took care of you. When I was too busy to do that, I would send her money, she didn't have time to work long enough to make very much."

What? I always thought I was from Adhara.

I examine him a bit closer. Why would he offer so much help, send money, if he wasn't my dad and was just a friend of a friend?

We have the same raven black hair, but our similarities end there. I don't have any traditional Cassiopeian features. Plus, my mom also had dark hair, I probably just got it from her.

"Anyway, she ended up getting a job in Adhara as a servant and took you with her. I didn't see either one of you for years after that."

He eyes me up and down differently than he has since I woke up. It's a loving look, with a touch of pride.

"You've grown a lot from that big, blue eyed baby that wouldn't stop giggling at every noise you heard. God, I still remember when you said your first words and when you took your first steps." A reminiscent smile touches his lips.

The way he's looking at me now, it's not a look I've ever gotten, and not one that I've seen often, but I recognize the feeling behind it.

"Why would you help my mom so much?" I ask, studying his features even closer. Not much about me looks Cassiopeian. Although tons of kids look more like one parent than the other.

"As I said, I was a friend of a friend. She was close to someone I was close with," he says. I watch him a bit longer, until his expression changes, as if he can read my thoughts. "I'm not your father, Isabelle. Believe me, if I were, I would've had you here with me, where it's safe. I would've never allowed your mother to let you stay in that palace with those people.

"A few years ago, eight by now, your mom was visiting Polaris to see family and dropped by Dominant Point to see me. On her way to find me she overheard a secret you know all about." A grim shadow briefly passes over his face.

"She told me what she heard and saw. I told her there must've been some kind of misunderstanding. She was terrified, she said she didn't think she'd even make it out of Dominant Point alive. So, even though I thought what she heard couldn't be true I made sure she got home safely, just to make her feel better. I was so sure it couldn't be true. Still, I did some digging on my own just to be sure.

"After I saw all I needed to know your mom was right, the current Cassiopeia representative saw what I was do-ing. I swore I wouldn't tell anyone. I was worried about what would happen because I knew, but it would've only been a couple more years before I would be included in this information myself, so I thought maybe they would be okay with me finding out early. A few days later, when your mom died-"

"*Died?* No, she didn't die. She ran away to make sure they couldn't find her." It's almost funny to me that he could've been so wrong about this. All humor comes crashing down when a shocked, sympathetic look takes over his face.

"I'm sorry. I didn't-I thought you knew. I didn't mean to tell you like this."

"But-no she- she left to make sure they *wouldn't* find her and she would be safe. She can't be dead." She just can't be. I could accept it when I thought she had just left me because maybe she wanted something else with her life. I don't know. But she was just trying to keep herself safe.

She didn't hate me. She didn't want to get away from me. I could've seen her again since I'm in hiding, too.

"They found her a couple of days after she reportedly disappeared. I took her back home to the Adhara palace after she heard Barret talking to the rest of the representatives. I offered to take her straight into hiding until I could be certain she had just misheard them but she said she needed to see you first," Kaito says.

I don't even remember the last day she was with me. I just remember when I realized she had been gone for a while. She must've been so terrified, and I didn't even notice.

Something in his expression tells me he isn't just sorry for me, he misses her too. I don't really care about that right now.

My cheeks are covered in flowing tears, my neck feels weird and damp, and my chin hurts from wobbling.

"I'm truly sorry, Isabelle. I didn't mean for you to find out like this. I'll give you a moment alone." He starts to push himself up from his chair.

"Wait." I try as hard as I can to sound normal, but still my voice shakes. He looks back at me. "I want you to finish what you were telling me." I wipe the tears off my face and neck.

"Are you sure? I think it would be better to give you a little time to–"

"No. I want you to finish what you were telling me." My throat feels raw with every word that comes out of it. He sits back into his seat.

"Very well."

He shifts around for a moment and clears his throat before continuing.

"When your mom...passed, I knew it must've had something to do with what she heard. I confirmed this on my own, and in doing so, I found out that my position in the outer layer of Dominant Point, training to join one day, did not give me the protection I thought it did.

"I grew a bit paranoid, waiting for when they would make an attempt on my life. So, I decided to spend some time in my estate in the countryside of my kingdom. But before we reached the edge of Polaris, where a ship was waiting to take me home, the car stopped.

"My driver had been sent by Dominant Point to kill me and make it look like a robbery. Thankfully, because of my paranoia I had a knife on me too. After a bit of a fight, I was able to take him down. I put him in my seat and set fire to the car. It burned so thoroughly that by the time it was found the only thing left of the new 'me' was my skeleton. Given that the plan was for me to die it went over smoothly with Dominant Point and I've been in Adhara ever since.

"Anyway, shortly after my 'death' I came to this place. I remembered hearing about it once, a space meant to be used for war hundreds of years ago before the creation of Dominant Point. Given its purpose, it was well hidden and thankfully, still standing strong. There's a reason this room doesn't have a window, the whole haven is underground.

"Very few people knew of this place. Before I came here I erased all documentation of it, this haven is completely lost to Dominant Point. I found more and more people who were either on the run from our government or simply needed a safe place and that's what this place has been. I've kept a close eye on the activities of Dominant Point from under their nose. That's how I knew the three of you were in danger.

"I apologize for the startling way that you had to be taken in, but we can't exactly go around with welcome flyers or politely converse with everyone we would like to take in. That's how we've stayed hidden for so many years. I hope you understand."

The revelation of how he survived all these years when the whole world is sure he was dead, when there's literally a body in his grave that people visit every year with flowers, should be shocking. But I honestly can't be brought to care all that much.

It makes sense. Dominant Point had sent out an order to kill him, and then there was an unrecognizable body in his seat of the car where he was supposed to be killed. Clean and tidy way to fake your death.

It also makes sense that Dominant Point wouldn't care to follow up with his assassin. Unless you're a royal, one of their own, or *about* to do something for them, they don't want to waste their time talking to you.

Something jogs in my memory.

"Are you the one that sent King Archer that warning letter?" If he managed to stay alive in secret for this long with other people, then surely he would have the resources to get information and spread it. Since he took care of me when I was a baby maybe that made him want to make sure I was okay.

He nods, "It was a big risk. We don't communicate with others–*especially* royalty– unless absolutely necessary. But helping two innocent teenagers seemed like a good cause."

I chew the inside of my cheek for a second, taking in all the information he's given me, then let out a breath.

"Okay."

"Okay? That's it?" His head crooks to the side.

"I want to see Ryder."

"You–alright then. I'm sorry but given Liam's reaction, I wasn't expecting such calm from you." I doubt Liam's reaction was anything like mine. For one thing, he hadn't just found out his mom has been dead for eight years. I imagine him with a gaping jaw, maybe even making an explosion sound with his mouth to show how 'mind blown' he is.

I don't say anything to Kaito as I get out of bed. He waits for me at the door of my room. From the looks of it, I would guess this room is just for medical purposes. He opens the door and I get a look at the place I was taken to while unconscious.

"This is our medical section. It's huge, which is nice should we ever need it, but the biggest injuries we typically see here are stubbed toes and kitchen incidents. For now, the amount of space we have is more than adequate, but should we get too many more people with us one day, we plan to convert some of the medical rooms into bedrooms," he explains with pride in his eyes as he walks us through the hall.

"How are you able to keep all this running on your own?" I ask. I know there are other people here, but unless more royals who are supposed to be dead show up, he's really the only one who could be in charge, he's the only one trained to be a leader.

He laughs at my question and shakes his head. "I couldn't. It would be impossible for one person to carry all this responsibility on their own. I'm in charge here, but I have a few other people that help me. Alex, Dain, and Kaspin. They help me lead, in addition to a few others we've picked up over the years. Dain was the first person to join me after I got here. He's watched this whole place become what it is. When–"

Someone stops in front of us, only briefly paying me any mind before turning to Kaito.

"Sir, Ryder is awake. He's angry, but he's no longer hostile."

"Perfect, thank you, Leon." Leon nods and steps back to unlock the door for us, then moves to wait outside.

"Let me see–" The moment Ryder's gaze lands on me, his face softens, then hardens again tenfold when he gets a good look at me. It must still be obvious that I was crying.

"What did you do to her?" Ryder yanks against his restraints, which I only now notice. I whip my head back towards Kaito.

"Why is he handcuffed? That guy said he wasn't being hostile." Kaito keeps his eyes on Ryder as he answers me.

"He broke both the arms of one of my men and tried to kill the one who had incapacitated you when we came to get you. I couldn't take the chance of him being a danger to any more of my people until I knew he was calm."

"Are you hurt?" Ryder asks me, his eyes sweeping over my whole body, searching for any sign of injury.

"No, no I'm fine. I'll tell you about it later." I try to reassure him. His eyes stay fixed on Kaito like he's ready to rip his head off. "Really, I'm fine." I turn back to Kaito. "How long until you're sure you can let him out? His reaction made sense, he thought you were going to hurt us."

"I'm not saying he was being irrational, I'm saying I have to think about my people's safety, and the two men currently getting medical attention would agree. I'll tell him what I told you, and then I'll make my decision from there," Kaito responds calmly.

"Okay," My feet stay planted firmly beneath me.

"This would be better to do without additional company. Would you please leave us for a moment? I bet Liam would love to see you. He had also been quite persistent about seeing you two." Kaito suggests. I'm not ready to leave Ryder yet, especially chained down.

"But—okay. I'll be back in twenty minutes though." I say, more confident than I feel. I'm aware that I'm in no position to make any demands and if Kaito says I can't come back in twenty minutes, I don't know if I'll be able to keep up my mock confidence.

"Of course, we'll see you then."

I don't want to leave Ryder right now, not at all, but the sooner Kaito can explain everything to him, the sooner he can be out of those cuffs.

Hopefully he'll also explain what happened to my mom so I don't have too. I speed walk to Ryder's bed and hug him tightly. He wraps his one free arm around me, pulling me in just as tight.

"I'll see you in a little bit," I mumble. He nods his head against me and releases his hold around my waist.

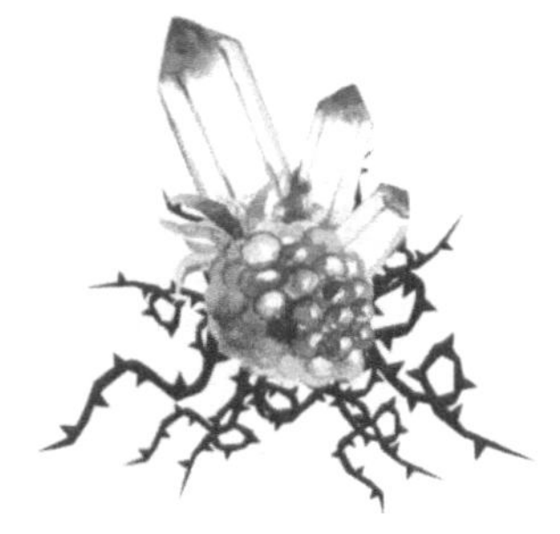

CHAPTER 21

ISABELLE

I take a few wrong turns when following Kaito's directions to the main hall, where I'm supposed to find Liam and dinner.

I pull my lip between my teeth, staring down the two splitting halls in front of me, unsure which way to go until I catch the distant sound of chatter from a large group of people.

Left hallway it is.

I follow the sound, growing louder and louder with each step down a long corridor of twists and turns. Laughter, conversation, and hushed murmurs guide me until I reach what I'm guessing is the main hall.

The room is large, with tall, stone walls moving into a dome overhead. There's a small fire pit in the center, a few benches around it, and towards the middle and outer part of the dome room are long rows of dining benches.

People are spread out across different parts of the room with trays of food in front of them. One side of the room has a line of people getting food scooped onto their trays. The wall behind them opens into a separated kitchen. There must be around two hundred people here.

I think I trust Kaito, and I believe everything he's told me, but I don't know any of these people, and every second that passes without seeing Liam makes my pulse pump louder and louder through my ears. Maybe I could go back to-

"Hey, there you are! I was wondering when they would let you out. Is Ryder with you or is he still being treated like a nut case?" Liam pulls me into an awkward side hug. I nearly jumped out of my skin before processing who was hugging me.

I've known him for as long as I can remember and I don't think we've ever hugged. But given the past day and

a half, depending on how long I was out, I would want to hug the first friendly face I saw too. So I wrap my arm around him for a moment before we pull apart.

"No, Ryder's not with me. Kaito's talking to him," I answer. Liam slowly nods his head.

"Ah, the old 'please don't try to kill any more of my people over a misunderstanding' talk. Also, I've been using my charming face and charismatic, irresistible self to get information. Nothing interesting or terrifying."

Liam typically isn't quiet for very long but I've noticed he talks even more when his nerves are high. I nudge his arm with my elbow.

"Are you okay?" I ask, ready for a sarcastic reply but figuring it's better to ask anyway. He shrugs his shoulders.

"I was a bit jumpy and convinced I was about to be handed over to Dominant Point to be murdered at first, but I opened my heart to them once they fed me. Speaking of which, they have these chicken wings and some cake that is just–*ugh*–to die for. I mean, not together, but-"

"I'm glad your stomach's satisfied but there are more important things to be thinking about other than the skill level of their cooks."

I whip my head around to see Ryder giving his brother the same look he always gives him. A mix of annoyance, 'what is wrong with you?', and 'how are we truly related?'.

I pull him into a quick hug, and by the time I pull away, his gaze has softened.

"How are you feeling?" I ask. I know he's spent the majority of his life being trained to take even the most unsettling situations in stride, but that overload of information should leave anyone's head spinning at least a little.

"I'm fine. I don't appreciate being tied down and sedated or being treated like *I* was the problem for hurting the ones who were abducting the people I care about. But I'm okay."

He shifts from his agitated tone, one that makes me think they probably shouldn't have uncuffed him so soon, to looking at me with sympathy.

"Are you alright?" he asks, taking my hand in his.

I know exactly what he's talking about, and now that I know I won't have to be the one to tell him about it, I don't wanna talk about it *at all.*

I just nod.

"I think we can trust them. I know the way they brought us here wasn't a good first impression, but given the fact that they've remained secret for years, it makes sense," I say.

Ryder makes an unsure face. "Are you sure? We can get out of here and still go to the cabin. This is–"

"I think she's right." Liam cuts in. "The only reason we have not to trust them is how they first got us here, but like she said, that does make sense. And everything Kaito said checks out too. Everyone I've talked to so far seems perfectly nice.

"And you're right, we can always go to the cabin but why do that when there's a chance we could be safe here? Spending the rest of our lives alone in the middle of nowhere sounds terrible compared to possibly being a part of a community we would be safe in." He doesn't make a single joke throughout his whole speech and doesn't say anything with even the touch of sarcasm. He's really thought this through and I think Ryder can tell. Ryder hesitates for a moment, considering, before speaking.

"That's part of my point. This does seem like a better outcome, or some kind of miracle happy ending and things that seem too good to be true usually are. This place seems safe until it isn't.

"What if tonight we fall asleep in our very own, new, plush beds, only to wake up being tied down in the kitchen because they're cannibals?" He shifts his gaze to me. "If you feel safe here and this is where you want to be, then I want that to happen. But I don't want to risk our safety, or our lives on something that could be an illusion." He gives me a pleading look, as if the decision is up to me.

I was ready to push for what I want, but I didn't think much would come of it. Instead Ryder's explanation sounds more like he is telling me why I *should* want to go, instead of why we *are* going, end of story.

"I want to stay," I say sternly. Ryder briefly shuts his eyes and Liam hides a small smile. "There's three of us to look out for each other if something does go wrong. We'll be cautious, but the chance of this actually being a safe place is worth it." At least Liam is on my side. I understand where Ryder is coming from, but I wouldn't be opposed to the idea of Liam and I ganging up on him until he yields and agrees to stay.

Ryder looks up at the ceiling for a minute, his lip caught between his teeth before looking back at me.

"Fine. We will stay here. But by the end of two weeks, if we aren't sure we can trust these people, we will leave. Okay?"

"Okay."

"Well, obviously, we would leave if in two weeks we still don't trust them," Liam says

He and I agree at the same time.

I spot Kaito across the room talking to some people, and hold out my hand to Liam and Ryder in a distracted, still wave "I'll be back later."

I don't hear what Ryder says, and I don't think I missed anything important when I don't hear what Liam says either. As I walk through the main hall, I take in all the people and smiling faces around me. It's amazing.

The whole world was supposed to be a victim of Dominant Point, but there are hundreds of people here with families and healthy children. Kaito was able to make an actual difference, saving so many people and bringing them to safety without Dominant Point even knowing.

He notices me before I reach him and turns away from the people he was speaking, a mother and a small daughter in her arms.

"Ah, Isabelle, how are you adjusting? I'm sure this is all very overwhelming." He shifts his body, subtly gesturing for me to walk with him. I follow him to the nearest table, taking a seat across from him.

"I'm okay. I wanted to ask you about something."

His brows lift slightly. "Go ahead."

"You were able to read Dominant Point's research on the sickness. What do you know about it?" I ask.

"Well, what specific parts do you want to know? I could show you the research I have saved in my office, but I imagine that would be boring when I could just narrow down what you want." He offers.

In this lighting, I see that he somehow looks twenty-three and decades past his thirty-six years of life all at once. His skin has maintained his youth, save for his smile lines. His hair is healthy with a few grays It's the look behind his eyes and the way he speaks, the way he carries himself in general, that ages him so much.

"I want to know more about where it started. I want to know what it is, not just the symptoms, if there's a cure or anything close to it, and why they decided to release it now. My mom's journal said that they would only use it if they needed to, if people decided to revolt over something, and I haven't heard of anything like that going on." I want to know everything, I want to see that research he thinks would be boring. He just nods.

"Why would they let you hear about it?" he asks.

"What? *Is* there a revolution happening?" I know I'm fairly isolated from the general population staying in the palace, but even in town there was nothing. Not until what they did to that poor old man, but that wasn't a revolution. They were attacking each other, not the government.

"No, not even close. Because if there were, you wouldn't know about it." I think he talks in puzzle pieces, or maybe I just don't understand because I'm not very educated. I wonder if he thinks I'm stupid for needing so much clarification, or if he does this on purpose.

"What do you mean?" I ask, heat creeping up my cheeks, making me feel small, like he would be laughing at me for not understanding. The look on his face isn't superior though, he looks happy to explain.

"Revolutions aren't a sudden big event born out of one moment. They build slowly. It's a collection of small outbursts over the course of years until people are desperate for change and tired of being ignored. It's like a fire that won't light very easily. One small spark can fizzle out, but, when people can hear about it, not just hear but really listen to why it happened, the sparks light up. If a man killed for something he believed in and the people were allowed to hear and speak about it without any censorship, they may decide he's not a murderer, he's a revolutionary.

"Events like this build up and *that's* how revolutions start. There's a reason the people aren't given the same resources as the royals. If you were able to talk to anyone at any time, that kind of news would spread like wildfire, completely uncensored. Of course, Dominant Point would never even let it get that far now. That was only an example. My point is, just because you haven't heard of something, don't think it isn't happening. Dominant Point released this sickness over little more than whispers of unrest."

If someone had started killing them that would be one thing, but they're doing this over whispers? Nothing even really happened. People just talk and they're killing inno-cent people because of it.

I can't understand how they could hurt so many people for nothing and not feel bad about it.

The old man, Iris, the man in the woods, that baby, the mother, everyone around them.

Dominant Point isn't just an organization, it's people. How could they ever do so much to so many people and be okay with it just because they were anxious?

I don't understand it. Nothing Kaito could explain could ever in a million years make me understand how someone can hurt another person and feel okay about it, let alone hurt thousands so intensely.

"What about the sickness?" I ask.

I won't ever understand this. I never want to be so full of hate I could even begin to. But I bet I could process whatever he says about the sickness a lot easier.

"The original patient, the one who Barret got his sam-ples from, worked in genetically modifying plants," he says. I know what genetics are, I know what it means to modify something, but I've never heard them put together in one phrase.

"How could he do something like that if he wasn't one of the royals? Or a member of Dominant Point? How would he have the technology?" Normal people have relatively the same kind of technology we did hundreds of years ago.

Royals can call someone all the way on the other side of the world and take pictures of things in less than a second. They can have a light on with the flip of a switch, although most prefer the look of candles. And Dominant Point has stuff that I wouldn't even think to imagine.

I don't know much about the first man to get sick but I know he wasn't a royal or a member of any layer of Dominant Point.

Kaito's eyes briefly light up at the chance to explain.

"He didn't have any kind of advanced technology. Genetically modifying plants can be done by simply splicing seeds together or changing agricultural habits. Actually, a lot of the fruits or vegetables you've eaten regularly at the palace come from a less intense form of genetic modification than what Gregor, the first infected, did," he starts talking a bit faster, although still not getting exactly to the point.

"The fruits and vegetables you eat have been slightly altered over centuries to be juicier or have smaller seeds. Did you know that an everberry doesn't exist on its own? It was a cross between a tart, sweet, bitter, yellow fruit and a juicy, sweet, red fruit-" He cuts himself off, a small redness blooming at the top of his cheeks.

"Sorry, I'm rambling. I just find the whole process interesting. Anyway, other than everberries, we don't have many other combined fruits, and we haven't done anything wildly groundbreaking in terms of changing our foods. Gregor did, though. He sold fruit and vegetables in his village and he was known for having the kind of things you couldn't find anywhere else, all grown in his backyard. From a blueberry that tastes like pineapple to things that were uniquely their own. One of his experiments, after breeding two plants that had gone through several generations of modification, and were nearly unrecognizable from the dozens of plants that went into them, is what created the virus.

"One theory is that since he lived right on the edge of the lake that feeds the glowing river, the strange algae may have had some effect. But there isn't much—or any— research on the algae. We're just told that's why the river glows. So it could've just been the combination of genes from many different fruits being modified. He tried the fruit and by that night, the doctor was watching his own body cut him from the inside out. The reason Dominant Point would've chosen this sickness over any other illness is how terrifying it is to watch. It destroys you even if you aren't one of the infected. That's what they wanted. Not just the population control, but the terror. Fear makes people obedient when they believe you are the one who ended something so vile and horrific.

"Gregor's wife, killed by Dominant Point, had told them about the plant when they asked. They took samples of it and discovered that while the berries held the sickness, the thorns held the cure." He seems almost more impressed by the complexity of the plant than by the amazing, wonderful, glorious thing he just said.

"There's a cure?" I confirm, my eyes widening. All we have to do is go to that man's property, with very thick gloves, and squeeze out the thorns. "Why haven't you collected it yet? Have you?"

The world's greatest issue right now and apparently we know how to end it. The whole world can be as at peace as the people in this room.

Dominant Point wanting me dead, the only life I've known being stripped away from me, and finding out my mom is dead just an hour ago, all of it seems insignificant compared to this news.

He shakes his head.

"They burned his whole property to the ground." He gives me a sympathetic look, flushing out my quickly sprouted hope.

"Oh." I should start waiting for him to finish explaining before I get all excited about seeing my mom or saving the world.

"But they did collect some. That's how they plan to end this once they think it's done enough for them. They have the cure, and they will use it as soon as it's convenient for them." He states.

"But how would they be able to cure more than a hundred people if it's only from the thorns of a plant grown on one man's property?"

He shrugs, "They duplicate it," he says, like it's the most obvious thing in the world.

"And what-"

"Would you like to see those files I told you about?" he cuts in, a small smile tugging at his mouth. "I'm starting to think I was wrong about them being boring."

CHAPTER 22

ISABELLE

One and a half hours later, after asking lots of questions and being surrounded by papers, I know enough to stop chewing my lip and making my head hurt from squinting my eyebrows together.

I know where it came from: a farmer who wanted to give people good food.

I know if there's a cure: only when Dominant Point decides there is.

I know how it really works, and I think I preferred it when my lip was chewed and I had a headache. It can work in two ways.

It can mutate the glucose in people's blood to form sugar crystals. They build slowly, starting as a small scrape on the inside of your veins, to slicing you apart from the inside out. Sometimes, they grow quickly enough to really burst through your skin. Other times, they grow so slowly that they cut you up inside until you bleed out without a single drop of blood ever leaving your body.

The other side of it targets parts of the brain like the hippocampus or amygdala, neither one of those I had ever heard of, or glucose. It causes hallucinations. Some people were reported talking to deceased loved ones, others terrified by monsters no one else could see.

People can either get the blood crystals, the hallucinations, or both. Some people are immune entirely, others are either immune to the crystals or the hallucinations. Although, Kaito says we don't know why some people are immune and others aren't.

Kaito offered to walk me to my room but I insisted I could find it myself. I told him I didn't want to take up any more of his time, but honestly, I just need a minute to myself. Although it's been more than a minute by now.

My room is two-zero-one, and there are plenty of signs pointing to which group of numbers are where, but I'm still lost.

I've somehow made it to the six-hundreds section without even noticing if I passed the two-hundreds. Maybe it's the other-

Right as I turn around, I slam into somebody. She stumbles back but still grabs my shoulders to steady me.

"I'm so sorry!" I blurt out. "That was my fault. I shouldn't have turned around like that in the middle of the hallway. I didn't think anyone was-"

"It's okay, really it's fine." she laughs. "It happens. No worries." She looks at me a bit closer, something seems to click behind her eyes. "You're Isabelle, right? You're new?"

"Yeah, that's me." I wonder if everyone here is told when new people arrive. I guess if two hundred people live underground together, word travels fast.

"Nice to meet you, Isabelle. How are you adjusting to everything? I know when I first got here it was like stepping into a living dream. It was amazing to feel safe but it took me a while to really believe it."

"Uh...it's been okay. Jarring, definitely," I say. She nods along with a friendly smile like she knows exactly how I feel. It's nice to imagine there may be someone else here who understands, besides just Liam and Ryder. I wonder if she was brought in unconscious too. "Actually, I'm a bit lost. Could you show me where room two-zero-one is?"

"Yeah of course. That's right on my way anyway. I'm room two-zero-two." She walks a few steps ahead of me before turning back and holding out her hand. "I'm Olivia, by the way."

"Nice to meet you, Olivia."

We talk a little as we make our way to our rooms. She makes this whole place feel a bit less scary.

I've decided to trust Kaito, if my mom did then so will I. But only really knowing Liam and Ryder and taking a leap of faith with Kaito is still nerve racking, despite what I told Ryder about feeling safe.

Olivia has white blonde hair, hazel eyes, a light dusting of freckles, and is a few inches shorter than me. Once we reach our doors, she stops me before I can go all the way into my room.

"If you ever want someone to sit with, I'll save you a seat," she offers.

"Thank you." I choose not to mention that I would never not be sitting with Ryder and Liam. Then she's gone, into her room. Maybe she'll sit with us sometime.

I hope Ryder is settling in here.

I take in the room around me and it's surprisingly nice. It's bare of any real decorations, but the bed is bigger than my old one, and there's even a night stand next to it.

The whole room is much larger than my old one but a closet compared to Ryder's. I'm sure that isn't helping with him settling in here either.

There are no windows, obviously, and an open door on the right side of the room leading to a small bathroom. The walls are a dull gray with no paint. The bed is pushed into the corner of the room. Every color is dull, and the room itself smells stale.

Still, I'm happy about it. I have my own space just for me and my own bathroom. The bathroom itself is pretty shabby, with a low toilet, an old looking sink, and a tiny shower. But I was imagining spending the rest of my life in a small cabin with two boys.

No matter how dull the room is, it's mine. And the thought of actually being safe here, of getting to stay is enough to pull me into a heavy, much needed sleep.

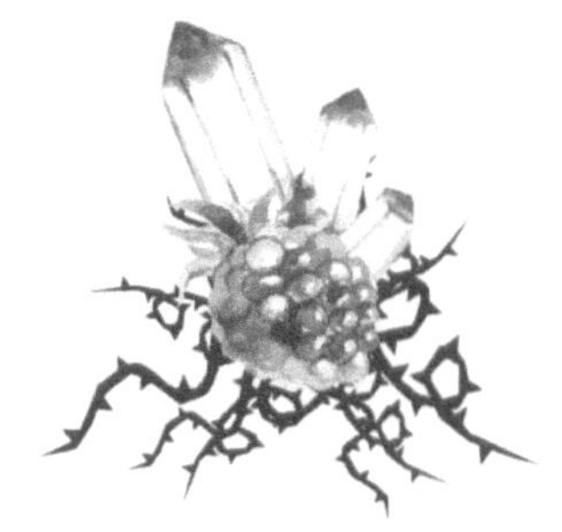

CHAPTER 23

It doesn't take me long to find my way from my room, three-eight-nine, to Kaito's office.

For whatever it's worth in terms of safety and security here, they make no effort to hide where certain rooms are. I knock on Kaito's door. As soon as his eyes land on me, they widen in surprise.

"Oh-Ryder, come in." He ushers me through the door and towards a chair at his desk. "What can I help you with? I know the rooms aren't in great condition, but I was hoping given the circumstances, even a prince could settle," he smiles an annoyingly pleasant smile. It seems so genuine, and if it's not, it could be dangerous.

"The dusty, stale room is fine. I wanted to talk to you about us being here. You say we're here as guests, meant to be protected, but waking up handcuffed to a bed gives me the strangest feeling that may not be the case." I plaster on a friendly smile to match his own.

He nods, "You were handcuffed because you were a danger to my people. You broke the bones of two of my men, and from the moment you woke up, you were just as hostile. It was for their protection. And I do mean what I said about you being safe here, as long as you're not a threat." He assures with a slight nod of his head.

"And you wanting us to stay has nothing to do with suddenly having two princes in your possession? From all these files it's clear you're a planner, albeit not a very organized one. Maybe one of your plans happens to involve a deal you could make using two direct heirs to the Adhara throne."

He laughs out loud. It's deep and mocking as he holds his hand to his chest. "I'm sorry," he says, composing himself with a sigh. "Do you have any idea what a massive offense it is to run away from the throne? I could walk back into my kingdom, alive and well, and I would still have no claim to anything. Same goes for you. There is very little value in either of us unless I kidnapped you and ransomed you back to your mother. But that would do me no good."

I raise an eyebrow at him. "Really? Being able to bargain with a queen would do you no good?" People would kidnap an infant for the chance to ransom a royal, people *have.*

"Why would I give up the safety I've built for myself and everyone else here over the years just for greed? We have everything we need, and most importantly, no one knows we exist. I would not throw that away in exchange for some fine, royal quality silk sheets."

He pins me with his gaze. "You are not a prisoner here, Ryder. If you would like I'll walk you to the exit right now. You'll be knocked out again and left miles away from us before you wake up. I have no interest in keeping you here, giving up the food that the people who appreciate this place need, if you are going to spend your time looking for enemies that don't exist here."

His brutally honest and careless tone while threatening to knock me out and dump me in the woods, miles away from here, puts me more at ease than any of his smiles or kind words.

"Okay," I say.

He looks taken aback for a moment at my cool tone.

"Although," I continue, "I would like to know why you've been making such an effort to convince us to want to stay. Letting Liam gorge himself on cake, showing Isabelle whatever research you had in here on the sickness just because she asked, why make such an effort if you truly don't care if we stay?"

He looks at me almost sympathetically. I hate it. I want to *strangle* him for looking at me like I would ever need his pity.

"Is it so hard to believe that I would want to help you feel more at ease?" he asks. "I do *care* if you stay, but not enough to fight you on it when I have people who want to be here that I need to take care of.

"I've taken care of Isabelle since she was a baby, and even if she doesn't remember, that means something to me. I watched her first steps and I soothed her when she cried. I would love very much for her to stay and to know that if her mother were watching over us, she would be happy to see her safe with me. But as much as I want that, it's entirely her choice. None of you have to stay, but I think you should and I hope you do. Although, I do also have a job for you and Liam eventually. However, you don't need to worry about that just yet."

I pause for a moment, taking in everything he's said.

"Okay." I agree. He still looks at her like the baby he took care of sixteen and a half years ago. I don't believe he would hurt her, or that he *wants* to hurt her. That doesn't mean he absolutely won't, but it does ease me.

I wouldn't go as far as to say that I entirely trust him with no room for doubt. But I don't fear for our safety. And I don't doubt that he would let me be knocked out and kicked to the curb should I ever ask.

The promise of being unconscious and laid down in the forest somewhere does make me feel better about this.

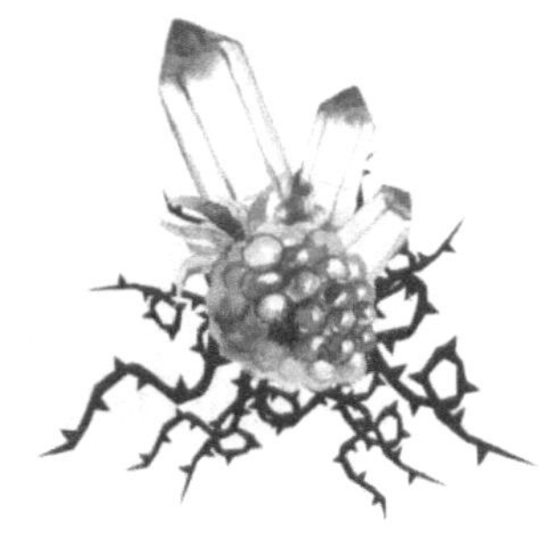

CHAPTER 24

ISABELLE

A light suddenly flicks on from the other side of my closed eyelids. Even with my eyes shut, it's too much. I roll over to my stomach and bury my whole face into the flat pillow. It's pitch black, and my blankets feel much better than they did when I was trying to fall asleep.

It's great until I need air again.

I kick the blankets off me and get out of bed. Since there are no windows, I'm guessing the whole place operates on the same timer for when the lights are on and off.

It's weird that they have automatic lights since they aren't a part of Dominant Point or still royalty. I guess that's the perks of having an ex-royal and an ex-almost Dominant Point member who knows how to install these kinds of things.

It doesn't take long for me to get ready, it's not like I have a long list of clothing options that I packed, and I only have the bare minimum for basic hygiene, which I would like to talk to someone about very soon.

By the time I open up my door, Olivia is walking away from hers.

"Hey!" I yell, much louder than I meant too. She turns around, startled. "Would you like to have breakfast with me and my friends?" The words slip out before I can second guess myself.

It may be a bit too straightforward after one conversation where she was nice to me. But I'm thinking that I may be here for the rest of my life. I'll never be safe being back out in the world and there's no reason to go to the cabin when I could be here. If I'll be underground for the next sixty or so years then I should at least try to make one extra friend.

And if she turns me down, I can be old and wrinkly next to Ryder and Liam knowing that at least I gave it a shot, and then never tried again.

She laughs away her startled expression, offering me the same friendly smile from last night. "Sure, I can point out which foods just look good but are actually gross. You'll never guess when you see them." After a few steps towards what I assume is the main hall, I got too turned around yesterday to tell, Olivia turns back to me, "Hey, do you mind if my boyfriend sits with us too?" she asks.

"Of course." I smile at her and a small smile lights up her face.

"Great, his name is Vance." She goes on for a bit about how nice he is and how we'll like him.

I know it's not a great way to start a friendship, but I'm only half listening. I don't really care about hearing how great someone that I've never met is.

Still, I smile, laugh, and nod when I should. The only experience I have with talking to other girls was with the other servants, and they were either much older than me or not interested in making friends.

Once we reach the main hall, it's packed with people lined up against the back with empty trays picking out scoops of food, while other people are just getting seated. Among them are Liam and Ryder.

"Over there." I say, nodding my head towards them.

"You save me a seat, I'll go get our breakfast trays." We break apart, and I head towards the only *truly* familiar faces here.

Liam's tray is covered in three pancakes, bacon, sausage, and a silver cup full of orange juice on the upper left side of the tray.

Ryder's tray is a more modest serving of the same, plus some fruit. I hope mine looks more like Ryder's, but with a lot more syrup.

"Are you the new paranoid one in our group?" Liam asks, grinning. "Syrup covered pancakes may not be doing great things for a person's health, but they're not poisonous."

"Someone I met last night went to get our trays," Both of them cock a brow up. As they sit in the same position, both with a fork in hand, and making nearly the same face I realize how similar and different they both look.

They're about the same height, but Liam has a broader, more muscular frame whereas Ryder's muscles are more subtle, strong but still lean. Liam's brownish-blonde hair contrasts sharply with Ryder's dark brown, nearly black hair. Liam's blue eyes and Ryder's green eyes stand as one of the only differences on their similar faces, both with a sharp jaw and strong cheek bones.

They look like the brothers they are in every way. Close enough to be made from the same genes and far enough apart to be nowhere near twins.

"Look at you already meeting new people."

"Who?"

Liam and Ryder ask at the same time. Their similarities mostly stop beneath the surface.

"Olivia." I answer Ryder, though a name wouldn't really tell him much, "I met her on my way out of Kaito's office. Her room's next to mine."

Ryder nods in acknowledgement as I swipe a few everberries off his tray and plop them in my mouth, remembering my talk with Kaito last night. Ryder subtly chews the corner of his lip, his eyes appearing lost in thought.

"Is everything okay?" I ask. He pulls his gaze back to my own before quickly shifting to look at something over my shoulder.

"Hi, I'm Olivia." She smiles at the two of them as she sets down a tray of cinnamon toast, fruit, bacon, and juice in front of me and another to the left of me.

"Is this how normal people feel when they meet Royals?" Liam asks, his voice dripping with playful sarcasm. Olivia gives me a confused look. "My name's Liam. This is my brother, Ryder. We've heard so much about you." My cheeks heat up.

"All I said was a girl named Olivia was getting my breakfast," I clarify. Her uncomfortable expression fades away as she smiles at them again.

"It's nice to meet you guys."

"Hey, Love." Olivia turns around and is swiftly greeted with a kiss on the cheek, from a guy I assume is Vance. His features are sharp, almost like a blade. Straight nose, strong jawline, cheekbones that could cut glass, and piercing, bright hazel eyes. He takes a seat next to Olivia, his posture rigid, as he looks around at all of us. "I'm Vance."

I watch the scene around us with an uncomfortable feeling crawling through me. Olivia being kissed on the cheek by her boyfriend. Families having breakfast together, smiling faces, and children running around the tables. It all looks so normal, so peaceful.

I wonder if most of these people even know how bad the sickness is, what it does to you, how it'll rip through your loved ones in front of you. I wonder if they would look like this if they knew how gruesome it is and then remembered that it's not a sickness doing this, it's people.

There are no more than two hundred people here, that's about how many people we saw at the village. Any of these people could've been among them instead of here. That mother and baby could've been here. All of those people could've been eating fluffy pancakes, dripping in syrup, like everything's okay. Instead they're lying in the dirt, dead.

I realize that there really is no rhyme or reason to who survives and who doesn't. Ryder and I were careful ever since the night King Archer came into my room. But maybe we're only alive because of dumb luck.

If I had seen a cute bunny and followed it just a few feet, maybe we would've gone through a slightly different path, one where we never pick up Liam, and one where we're never found by The Haven.

Right now, we could be watching each other get torn apart from the inside out.

I wonder if Kaito has any plans to help the people who got unlucky, who saw a cute bunny. Or if he'll take in the lucky few while the rest of the world is tortured by the people they trust.

Vance, Olivia, and Liam talk for a bit while Ryder stays quiet. I inhale my food, barley tasting any of it. I didn't have a chance to eat last night.

"What's wrong?" I ask, leaning slightly across the table and lowering my voice. Ryder looks over at everyone talking next to us before bringing his gaze back to mine.

"Can we talk in private?" he whispers.

"Of course." I take a couple final pieces from my tray as I stand up with Ryder. He leads us down the closest hallway leading out of the main hall until we're in a shadow covered, semi-private space.

"I know we agreed to stay here, and I think you were right. I do believe that we're safe here, but I need to find a way to contact my mother, and that may mean leaving." He whispers.

I wait for him to continue, to say that while he would like to do that, he obviously wouldn't because it's dangerous and crazy, but he doesn't.

"What? No! You can't leave after *agreeing* that it's safe here. The most powerful people in the world want you dead, and going back to the palace is the worst thing you could possibly do."

He purses his lips together. "I know. And for the record I don't plan on getting caught or staying gone. I just need to find a way to send her a message. I need to tell her that Liam and I are okay and we love her."

"But-"

"It was one thing to accept never seeing her again when we first left, but after what Liam told us when he first joined us and the fact that both her children are gone, I can't sit by and know she's suffering. I need to do something, I need to."

Ryder's mom has always been close with both of them. She was the warmth to their father's cold. While Henry never treated them as anything more than what they would one day be, their mother actually loved them. Since they knew what it felt like to be unloved by a parent, they've both cherished that.

"I know you want to help her. I understand that, but think about what she would want if she knew everything. I'm sure she would love to hear that you're safe, but more than anything she would want you to actually *be safe*. That means not trying to send messages to anyone in the palace. It's too risky. Please, at least consider that doing nothing may be best. Please." I beg.

The tension builds in my muscles with every second he's silent.

"We can talk to Kaito," I offer, trying to keep my voice steady. "He's been keeping track of the royals and Dominant Point's every move for years. Maybe he'll have some way that you can safely get a small message to your mother."

"She-" he starts but I cut him off.

"At least just talk to Kaito first. And if he doesn't have any way to send her a message, which I doubt, please, please *consider* not giving her one at all."

He drags his hand over his face. He hardly ever lets himself to show such visible signs of stress, seeing it now makes my stomach twist.

"Okay." He agrees, reluctantly. "I'll talk to Kaito and if he can't do something, then I'll let it go. I won't contact her on my own." He finally relents.

I wrap my arms around his neck and pull him down into a hug. He freezes for a second. My heart aches to think about what he must be feeling before he wraps his arms around me, his fingers digging into my back, as he pushes his face into the crook of my neck.

We've hugged each other at least a million times in our lives, but none have felt like this. So intimate, full of unspoken understanding. Silently telling me how much he's hurting.

I run through all the things I could say to him.

I love you, the same words we've said since we were kids suddenly don't feel like enough.

I understand, but I don't. I would if his mom were dead but I don't understand what this feels like.

It's going to be okay, yeah, eventually he'll come to terms with never seeing his mom again, with knowing that she'll spend the rest of her life missing her children and never knowing why they left. But it's not okay right now, so why pretend that doesn't matter just because one day it might hurt less?

So I say nothing, and we hold each other until my muscles hurt.

CHAPTER 25

RYDER

Isabelle and I follow Kaito back to his office. She started looking for him as soon as we pulled away from each other. After no more than five seconds of her explaining what we wanted he cut her off, which I did not appreciate, to say we should speak in his office.

"I try to be completely transparent about anything important or dangerous going on," Kaito drones as he flips through a ring of keys, "but I prefer not to speak about it out in the open. I've found that it tends to make people feel like there's no escape from the threat of Dominant Point, and less like this is the haven it's meant to be."

I glance to my left at Isabelle, who looks just as worried as if it were her own mother we were trying to contact. Since we were old enough to understand that we weren't the only people in the world, she's always been the kind of friend to treat a loved one's problems as her own.

As someone who loves her, it worries me how deeply she cares for other people, sometimes to the point of neglecting herself. But as someone who's loved *by* her, it's a rare comfort to know she truly, wholeheartedly cares.

Her raven black hair looks healthier than it did in the palace, most likely due to whatever new products they've supplied her with. I've hated mine, but I'm accustomed to the best. Plus I'm a bigger fan of rose and lilac over lavender.

She looks thinner, too. I shouldn't have pulled her away from breakfast earlier.

Beyond the clear signs of malnourishment from days spent walking for hours with minimal rations, she's still the same black haired, pale skinned, and dark blue eyed girl I used to steal sweets with, to eat under the stars on the rooftop where no one would think to find us.

Kaito gestures for us to take the two chairs in front of his desk as he sits down. "Okay, now continue what you were telling me."

This time, instead of jumping straight to it, Isabelle stays silent and turns to me. I shift a little in my seat before answering.

If my father had seen such an obvious sign of emotional discomfort, no matter how subtle, it would've been a very unpleasant night ahead of me.

"My mother isn't doing well, and I would like to send her some sort of message, however vague, to tell her that my brother and I are okay."

Isabelle reaches over to give my hand a quick squeeze, never taking her eyes off of Kaito's face.

Never seeing my mother again is something I can accept. I was willing to the moment I left the palace with Isabelle. Even before then, I knew once I was sent to Dominant Point, my visits with her would become rare.

What's eating me alive now isn't the idea of losing her, it's knowing how badly she must be hurting.

I had expected her to be sad about my absence for a short while, but eventually she'd move on, tuck my memory away to the back of her mind, and go on with life. Hearing what Liam said about how miserable she was felt like a hard punch to the gut. And knowing she's living through that pain twice, with both her sons gone, that's the part I can't let go of.

Kaito draws in a long breath, pressing his lips together as he looks down at his desk. With a heavy sigh, he lifts his gaze back to mine.

"No."

"How can you not have any way to contact her?" Isabelle asks, her voice sharp. "You've been tracking everything they do, undetected, for years. You must be able to do something."

"I can, but I won't. I truly am sorry about what your mother must be going through, Ryder. But messages get intercepted all the time. That's half of how I get my own information. I cannot risk that happening now and endangering everyone here, not for the sake of someone's feelings."

My fingers clench and unclench around the arm rests, trying to anchor myself. I can feel Isabelle's gaze burning through me, but I can't bring myself to look at her. I rise silently from my seat and head for the door. I don't trust myself to say anything to Kaito right now and not get us all thrown out.

I pull the door shut behind me, but before it can latch Isabelle pulls it back open as she follows me.

"I'm sorry," she says softly, reaching for my hand, like an anchor to hold onto.

"It's not your fault. Besides, it was a good idea." She lets go of my hand to quickly step in front of me, stopping me in my path.

"Please don't try to contact her on your own. I know it's hard but she'll be okay. She still has your dad, and for all his faults as a dad, he's always been a great husband to her. Liam and I are here, and we need you to stay safe." She's only inches from me, as if should she step away even a little, I'll bolt for the first exit and run towards the palace myself.

I place both my hands on her shoulders, "I promise. I won't make any attempt to contact her on my own." She releases a steady breath, and I feel her shoulders relax under my palms. I've never broken a promise to her before and I haven't made many.

She steps back to my side and follows me hand in hand back to my room. When we first started having sleep overs, it was after the first time she saw fresh blood on my back.

My father had been watching one of my lessons. It was about wilderness survival, and that day's lesson was teaching me to grind up a specific bug to use as an antibiotic on open cuts. It's proven to prevent infection and speed healing. When they brought me a small dish of still living bugs to be crushed, I refused. My father stepped in, and after much insisting, he had me grind up all of them as I cried.

To say the least, he was unhappy with my blatant show of weakness, and later that night he had a servant, the one whose room is right next to Isabelle, beat my exposed back with one of my fathers belts. If he was in a particularly foul mood, which eventually became quite often, he would do it himself.

We were around five and seven years old when she saw that first cut, and I've made somewhat of an effort to hide any new ones since then. Unless we're swimming in the river, in which case we choose not to talk or think about it.

That was how our slumber parties started. She insisted on staying with me because while she would get in trouble if caught in the prince's room at night, especially as we got older, at least he wouldn't hurt me while she was there.

Over time, we stopped thinking of them as necessary and just enjoyed each other's company. Now, over ten years later, she spends the night in my room to protect me from a different kind of hurt.

And just like before, even if there's nothing she can do to stop what's happening, she really does help.

CHAPTER 26

ISABELLE

I woke up in Ryder's bed with our limbs tangled together, with just about an hour left until dinner time. We talked, played hand and story games, until eventually we slept the day away. There goes my sleep schedule.

The signs in the hallway are finally starting to make more sense to me, and thanks to the map Kaito gave me. I made it back to my room without a single wrong turn.

"Oh, hey, Isabelle!" Olivia calls out as she's leaving her room.

"Hi." I wave awkwardly.

"I'm so glad to see you. I was wondering if since you didn't have much with you when you came here, would you like to take a look at some of my clothes? You could pick out a few things you might want? I think we're around the same size."

"Oh–sure–yeah, that would be great. Thank you."

She smiles and steps aside, opening her door wider for me to come in. Clearly abandoning whatever she was planning to do when she left her room.

Her room has the same basic layout as mine, as if they may have once been identical, but hers has life to it.

The walls are still the same dreary color, but hers are covered in hand painted pink and yellow flowers. Her sheets are as dull as mine and her bed is in the same place, but her night stand is overflowing with hand made crafts. And while my closet is empty, spare for a few hangers that were already there and my bag stuffed into the back corner, hers is bursting with color and fabrics.

"I've got way more than I ever wear," she says, dragging out the first armful of clothes and dropping them on her bed. "So just tell me if anything catches your eye and I probably won't mind parting with it."

I start sorting through the pile of shirts, shorts, pants, skirts, and lots and lots of dresses.

"When they came to get me I was still in my own house, so they brought my whole closet with them. Since we don't have tons of new clothes coming in often or much in terms of decoration around here, it was really nice to have something that let me express my own style. A few painted flowers can only do so much to make a space feel like it's really *yours*. You know?" She picks up a handmade paper flower and rolls the stem between her fingers. "Although, I do get lots of crafts to decorate with from volunteering with the kids."

I can see what she means by wanting to express herself.

Her clothes look like they could belong to people living a thousand different lives. It makes it hard for me to guess what her life was like before this place.

How people dress typically reflects the life they live. As servants, we're given a single black long sleeve jumpsuit. The royals often dress extravagantly in silks and crystal covered clothing. On special occasions they wear the large dresses that would be seen in paintings from centuries ago, only now with even more sparkle. For the most part they wear a simple silhouette dress or suit with wonderful fabric and intricate designs.

Except Ryder's mom. She loves the truly regal gowns, the kind that shimmer when she walks and flows wide from her hips. They always made it the most fun to sit on her lap while she read stories to Ryder, Liam, and me. She was like a big cushion.

Warriors, and anyone working in a combat related role, typically wear all black. Their outfits are made up of tight, comfortable looking pants, long sleeves, and various straps and belts to hold weapons. The women often wear an ankle length skirt with a high slit all the way up. Like a blend of graceful beauty and fierce strength.

Townspeople wear a variety of silhouettes, all made of dull fabric. Long dresses, short ones, skirts, jackets, and some women even wear pants. Although that's mostly for the women working jobs that require more mobility.

It's cheaper to have a single garment serve as a whole outfit rather than needing both a shirt and pants. It's also easier to make cheap dresses look nice.

The only fabric most people have access to is a dull, dreary color, and rarely comfortable. But, people turn it into something beautiful.

They buy cheap, plain clothes and cover them in colorful, unique embroidery. No two outfits end up exactly the same. If they can afford a lot of thread, they're beautiful. Some only manage to get enough thread for one or two embroidered details, even then it adds up to something unique and special. The styles vary from kingdom to kingdom, each with its own patterns, colors, and meanings.

Olivia's clothes are a beautiful mix of all of them.

"What did you do before this?" I ask.

"My dad was a small-time designer." She says with a smile, "I liked almost every style of clothing, as long as it was done well, so he made me lots of everything. Most of this stuff doesn't really make sense. Those are the ones I drew up myself and insisted would look good if he just made them. I was obviously never going to follow in his footsteps." She laughs.

"Is your dad here too?" I ask.

Her smile falters. "No, he's not."

She quickly looks over the pile of clothes and grabs the first thing that catches her eye. "You should try this on," She says, holding up a long white dress covered in embroidered blue flowers with a deep neck line, and delicate stitching.

It's not something I would've ever worn before, and something nice enough that I would've only seen it a couple times in town.

I reach out and rub the fabric between my fingers, tracing over the bumps of flowers. The white fabric is so *soft*. I could wear this as pajamas.

After trying on that dress and several other clothes, I leave Olivia's room wearing the blue flower embroidered dress and my arms overflowing with fabrics. I took a couple of blouses, some skirts, a brown fur coat, a pair of jeans, a pair of gray cotton pants, and many, many dresses.

It feels wrong to be getting so excited about some clothes when I know people are suffering in ways that make me think everyone who believes in a higher power or some God must be wrong. How could a good God allow this much pain to exist?

But selfishly, I still smile as I walk out of her room, my fingers drifting over each of the different fabrics.

It feels really nice to talk to another girl like this. My only true friend for most of my life has been Ryder, and I guess now I would consider Liam a friend too, but I've never been truly close with another girl.

Not that it was on purpose. I actually think girls are really fun to talk to. I was just never that close with any of the servants, and I don't know many people outside of the palace.

It feels different. Good. Like having a friend who could *really* understand you if they get to know you enough. I hold the clothes extra tight as I hang them up delicately in my closet.

My first gift from my first girl friend.

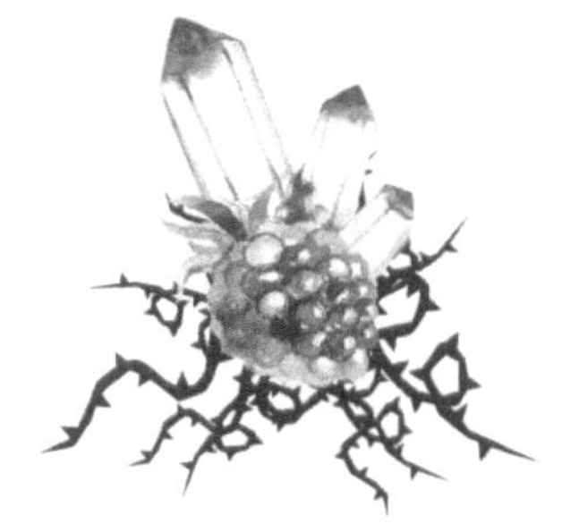

CHAPTER 27

RYDER

Isabelle came into the main hall side by side with Olivia, wearing a beautiful dress I'm sure she's never worn before. It's a soft looking white fabric covered in tiny embroidered blue flowers that set off her black hair so beautifully.

The hem brushes the top of her feet, and the v-shaped neckline dips as low as it can before tapering into loose short sleeves. I've rarely seen her in anything but her black uniform or pajamas and she is absolutely glowing.

She sits across from me now, deep in conversation with Olivia, and I can't seem to focus on a single word Olivia's saying. An ear to ear smile has been on Isabelle's face since the moment she walked in.

With her long black hair twisted into a braided crown, bright smile, and beautiful dress, she looks like someone I'd see in a painting hanging in the palace halls.

A princess from a hundred years ago not nearly dressed up enough for a royal portrait, yet somehow more beautiful than any other one lining those grand walls.

I've known she was beautiful our whole lives. Long black hair, full lips, dark blue eyes, and that faint scar across her cheek. How could anyone not find her beautiful?

It's just never been something I've felt so strongly before. There were always other things about her to notice and adore, the things that made her my best friend, not just the beautiful servant.

Seeing someone who's beautiful is common. Knowing someone who makes you feel like, if soulmates come in all forms, even those who are only ever friends, then this is my person. That's special. That's how I've always known Isabelle.

For most of my life, I've been able to look at her and see the body and face that carries my best friend's soul. But when I do take in what she looks like, it's breathtaking, excruciating. Like nothing that existed before has ever been truly beautiful because it wasn't her.

Olivia turns her attention away from Isabelle as soon as Vance sits beside her. Isabelle gives him a kind smile, but it's less sincere than the one she's been wearing all night.

"Anyway, I just don't feel like I was being an asshole if I didn't even know," Liam says, way too close to my ear.

"What are you talking about?" I ask, already annoyed. He stares at me, incredulous, then rolls his eyes.

"Have you been listening to anything I've been saying?"

"No."

"I was telling you—never mind."

"Good."

"Well, thank you for leaving all the kindness in mother's womb and saving it all for me. I'm a ray of sunshine, you're a dick."

"I don't know what you were telling me, but I don't think a ray of sunshine needs to defend the fact that he's not an 'asshole'."

"Whatever." He rolls his eyes.

Isabelle reaches across the table to pick off bits from my tray, reminding me why I had been wanting to see her so badly.

My thoughts had gotten a little sidetracked after she walked in. I look down at her tray to make sure I'm not taking her away from another full meal before asking.

"Isabelle, will you come with me for a walk?"

She looks up at me and pauses with her mouth open, a roll halfway past her lips. She quickly pops it in her mouth and stands.

"Yeah, of course."

As soon as we're out of ear shot from everyone else, a more sympathetic look settles over her face.

"What did you want to talk about?"

"Nothing, nothing's wrong," I reassure her. She relaxes and I realize she was probably only so quick to agree because of what happened earlier today.

"I spent a while walking around The Haven after you left and I found something I thought you might want to see."

"What is it?" She asks.

I fight back a smile, "You'll see."

Also, if we get caught I want her to have plausible deniability that she didn't know what I was planning.

I lead us through a maze of twists and turns in The Haven's tunnels until we reach a door.

"Fire escape?" she asks, reading the sign on the door.

"They won't lock it in case there really is a fire and the person with the key doesn't make it in time." She pulls me back as I reach out for the handle.

"You want to leave?"

Her brows knit together as her face twists into a look of betrayal. It's a painful expression to watch.

Her grip on my wrist tightens as if she plans to keep me here through pure physical strength alone.

"No, I don't want to leave. I want to show you something." I reassure her, opening the door to the fire escape and stepping to the side, waiting for her to come forward towards the ladder. "It's not a long climb, and the latch at the top is easy enough to open."

She looks at me with a weary expression for a moment, then starts to climb. Once the door is shut behind me I see her visibly relax, no longer afraid of being caught.

"Just twist the lever to the left, then push up," I instruct once she reaches the top. The door is covered on the surface by a fake, nearly weightless rock, surrounded by a scatter of real ones.

She pushes it open, then freezes before scrambling the rest of the way out. By the time I'm on the surface beside her she's staring out at the view in front of us.

"It's beautiful," she whispers.

The Haven lies deep beneath a cliff overlooking the beach. Behind us, moss covered trees with low hanging limbs stand tight together, creating a peaceful, hidden space from the rest of the world. Beneath our feet, a colorful wave of flowers bleed into pale sand. Rocks covered in bright shells rest packed together on one side of the water, the other side stretches out into open water of wave after uninterrupted wave.

It's beautiful, breathtaking even, but nothing compared to how it looks reflected in her eyes.

She takes a seat at the edge of the cliff, dangling her feet over the edge.

"This is nothing like the view from our spot in the palace," she says.

"Is it better?" I ask, sitting down beside her.

"I'm not sure."

She leans her head on my shoulder. I'm not sure either, and I think that we both have more in mind than how the view looks.

Our spot in the palace was ours alone, a hidden escape from everything and everyone around us. This is the same, but also entirely different.

"I'm sorry about your mom," she says.

"Me too."

I wrap my arm over her shoulder and pull her in closer, deeply grateful for the first real moment of privacy we've had since arriving here.

"Of all the people I could've had to leave my life with, I'm glad it was you." I whisper.

She nudges me so we fall side by side with our backs to the grass and our feet dangling over the cliff's edge. Her head rests in the crook of my neck and her arm drapes across my torso.

I've never been so grateful to have someone who can offer so much comfort, so much understanding, without a single word needing to be spoken.

Her lying here beside me, with the gentle breeze stirring the smallest strands of our hair and swaying the grass around us, feels like an impossible moment of calm. Here, no matter how unlikely it seems, I can believe that everything will be okay.

We kissed once when we were kids. We were about seven and nine years old and didn't understand yet how much a kiss could mean.

She had just been saying thank you for the dress I had made for her. Later on, I knew it didn't count, afterall we were just kids. A kiss for a gift.

She pulls away to look up at me.

"I used to think about what it would be like to be a servant for the rest of my life. And I'd think that at the very least, I'm glad I got to be with you before you would've left." I watch the curve of her soft, pink lips form each word, "Do you remember when we were little and I first realized the difference between why you lived in the palace and why I did? You had that beautiful, blue silk ball gown made for me.

"I wore it for days before my mom finally convinced me to change out of it. You made me feel like someone important in a beautiful dress. I want you to know that moment still means a lot to me." I can feel her gaze burning into me, but I can't bring myself to look into her eyes and away from her lips.

Absently, I barely even feel my words come from my mouth.

"You would be someone important even if you wore rags." I mindlessly pull myself closer to her, my lips towards hers, until I feel her freeze in my arms.

I pull back right away, pleading with the ground to swallow me whole.

Just as I shut my eyes, cursing myself, I feel her lips quickly brush mine. My eyes shoot back open to look at her, and she looks just as wary as I did. Her eyes are wide, her forehead slightly tense, with her bottom lip tucked between her teeth.

It was a quick kiss. So light that if she told me I'd imagined it, if she said it was only the wind brushing my lips, I would believe her. But it still tells me everything I needed to know.

I crash my lips to hers.

I move so I'm on top of her. Her hands immediately find a place in my hair and behind my neck. Her fingers run through my hair as she pulls me closer. Her touch is both gentle and desperate, in sync with the way her lips move with mine.

My hands caress the dip of her waist, feeling the smooth fabric and delicate bumps of embroidery on her new dress. Touching her like this is absolutely intoxicating.

Her taste, her feel, the way she moves beneath me, it's like discovering a new favorite thing about the home you've loved for years.

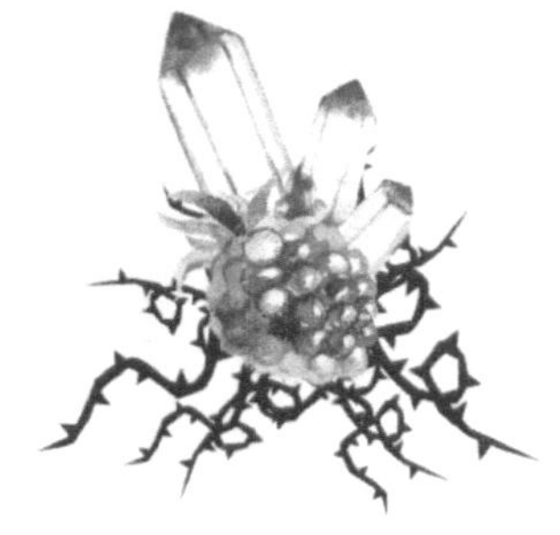

CHAPTER 28

RYDER

Everything feels lighter as I walk through the halls. For a few moments up there, the weight of what's happening to my people, the trapped feeling that comes from knowing there's little I can do about it, was briefly lifted off my shoulders. Having it be just the two of us, like it's always been, put a pause on everything else. She's like my own medicine.

When I'm with her, there's only her. Everything else we may be going through at any given moment just drifts away into background noise, even if only for a few mo-ments.

I'm also aware that I have someone else to thank for my new found sense of calm. It never stays long, but for every chance I do get, I owe it largely to Isabelle—and a small part to someone else.

I won't drag it out or make it sappy in the slightest. I may no longer be a prince but I am still above certain un-princely behaviors, overbearing apologies and excessive gratitude being two of them. A simple apology for my earlier behavior and a brief thank you for the hospitality will suffice.

I make it to Kaito's office and knock. There's no sound of movement from the other side of the door. I adjust my shirt, smoothing out any wrinkles while debating whether I should knock again. A prince doesn't stand outside someone's door, waiting to say thank you, and certainly doesn't wait long enough to knock again, as if his time is more important than mine.

It's the thought that counts. And I *thought* about saying thank you. That's good enough.

I start to turn away, but stop. The idea that I shouldn't even stoop low enough to apologize and thank someone, let alone wait outside their door, only came from my father.

I raise my fist to knock once more. Doing something my father explicitly taught me not to do, doing what feels right instead, and doing it on my own feels good, but still uneasy.

Before my knuckles hit the door, I catch him out of the corner of my eye.

He takes long, certain strides down the hall. I follow after him. Just as I get close enough, he rounds another corner. My desire to thank him for providing us with shelter and safety despite my prickliness in the beginning is now greatly outweighed by my curiosity to see where he's walking with such purpose.

I take the same turn he did, staying close to the wall in case I'm not meant to see where he's going. And I suspect I'm not.

By the time I'm around the corner, less than five seconds after him, he's gone. I look down every hall leading away from here. They're all completely straight with nowhere to hide.

He's just...gone.

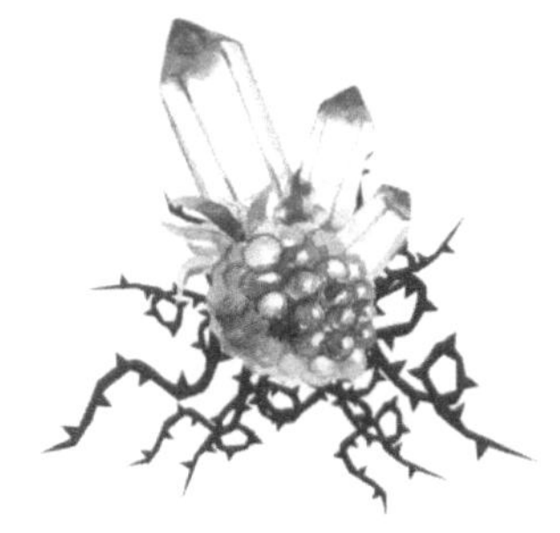

CHAPTER 29

ISABELLE

"**I** knew it!" Olivia kicks her feet against the side of her bed, "I knew there was no way you two were just friends!" She grins ear to ear like she just solved a puzzle no one else even knew existed.

A blush heats my cheeks.

I hadn't even fully realized how much I wanted him as more than a friend until he kissed me.

Then it just kind of snapped. Like finally figuring out something you didn't even realize you'd been asking. It just felt so right.

It made sense of the way my eyes lingered on him a little longer when he wasn't looking, or how my stomach had twisted when he got his first girlfriend.

Ryder and I stayed out on the surface, going back and forth between kissing each other and lying beside each other until the only light was from the stars and the moon.

When I finally got to my room, I knocked on Olivia's door instead of my own and I've been giving her every detail since then.

How his hands were firm yet gentle. How I had seen him watching my lips before we kissed. How perfectly his lips fit with mine and how deeply I missed his taste every time we pulled apart for air.

It was incredible. It gave every romance book I've read in the palace library a whole new meaning.

Still, it's hard to put everything I'm feeling into words, especially when I'm not entirely sure what I'm thinking. It feels impossible for a kiss to mean so much, given everything happening outside of this place. But somehow it does.

It's so new, but still so, so right. I feel ridiculous for ever believing the way I loved him was only platonic.

Of course he would mean more than that to me. Noth-ing's ever been so stupidly obvious in my life.

"Okay, enough about me and Ryder. What about you and Vance?"

"What about me and Vance?" She blushes. For a second, I almost wonder if I made a mistake, if maybe this isn't what girlfriends talk to each other about, but the wide, bashful grin on her face quickly pushes that thought away.

"You like him?" I ask. She rolls her eyes at my dumb question.

"Well, he's my boyfriend, so yes, I like him." She laughs.

"You were acting like you wanted to talk about my one kiss for hours, but that's all you have to say when it's about you?"

She laughs, then pauses, sucking her lip between her teeth as she searches the ceiling for the right words.

"Vance was like...Before I came here, I lived with my dad. Our house was on the outer side of town in a quiet but beautiful place. When Dominant Point first planted the sickness, he was the first person to get it anywhere near us. No one else had heard about it and no one was willing to try to help. They were all too afraid of getting sick. It didn't matter anyway. Most of them are dead.

"I spent four days taking care of my dad. I watched bruises form across his whole body. I watched him lose the ability to move, even to talk. All he could do was groan and even that was painful. He bled from his eyes like tears. His nose, his mouth, his ears were so bloody I could barely see what pattern on the blankets used to be. Eventually, a small crystal split up from his wrist and he died."

She pauses, her eyes trailing off into a distant place. She swallows and looks down at her hands.

"I spent another two days after that tending to his corpse like he was still alive. I forced food and water down his throat. I just kind of convinced myself he was still alive and the only reason he stopped moving or talking or breathing was because it hurt. I spent all day and night lying next to his body, holding him. I just–I didn't want him to be gone." Her voice cracks as tears well up in her eyes. She quickly wipes them away then continues.

"Turns out I'm lucky, I'm immune. Everyone else in my village was dead. Some scouts from The Haven found me in my house, still curled up next to my dad's corpse. His lifeless, open eyes already looked terrible and he was starting to smell dead too. They took me back here.

"This was only a couple of weeks ago, but it feels like months. When I first got here they told me about Dominant Point's role in all this, and I just kind of broke. I was convinced nothing could ever be good again. That there was nothing in this world that could make up for fathers dying in front of our eyes and our government being responsible for it all without a shred of remorse.

"Vance was like my proof that good things could come after bad ones, no matter how awful. We haven't been together long, so I won't say I love him. I know that would be ridiculous. But he's the one who showed me that things can still be good enough to make life worth living, even with all the bad stuff."

A small, thoughtful smile pulls at her lips, even as tears stream down her face. She quickly and messily wipes at them.

"Sorry, I didn't mean to get all sappy. Just, including how I felt when I got here helps explain how much he means to me."

"Are you okay?" I ask. I don't know how she could be. Even if she's coping or found someone to give her hope, no one is just *okay* after that. I just want her to know she has someone besides her boyfriend too.

Her bows crease in the middle, like she's been fighting to hold her face together to keep from sobbing. Her lip and chin wobble as she tries to get the words out, getting too choked up each time.

"I miss him," her voice cracks. "He made me pancakes every week and would save up all week long for the ingredients. He made me all the clothes I wanted. He told me he would give me more love than any other kid with a dad *and* a mom, so I wouldn't miss out on anything. He was a good man and an amazing dad. He–he had the sweetest smile that would–that wrinkled his whole face. I want every single person in Dominant Point dead and I want them to be afraid when it happens."

She finishes. Her eyes are distant, like she's watching it all play out in her mind. Watching every representative understand what's about to happen to them. And if there's a hell, she wants them to *know* it's waiting for them.

"I dream about it," she whispers. "I dream about the moment they find out someone's coming for them. How they'll be so certain they're not in real danger, how they'll laugh at the people attacking them for ever thinking they could win against Dominant Point. And then the look on their faces when they realize they're going to die.

"How they'll *beg* for mercy, for forgiveness from whoever gets to kill them. Someone who's spent years feeling so strong, so much better than everyone and he'll be sobbing on his knees, begging with snot bubbles coming out of his nose like a pathetic mess, pissing himself because he's so afraid. And every last one of them will be killed, one by one, so the others know there's nothing they can do to stop it. Just like the rest of the world could do nothing to stop what Dominant Point did to them."

The image she painted...it feels good to imagine. It feels *right,* even if I know it's wrong to want to hurt someone so badly.

But after everything they've done, after everything I've *seen* them do, their pain, their death is the only thing that's right.

I think of that mother and baby. The old man people killed out of fear for what Dominant Point did to them. Iris. What almost happened to Ryder. Almost to Liam. Olivia's dad. And suddenly, the picture Olivia painted looks like the only right thing.

They need to be afraid. They need to understand what they've done to people who didn't deserve it. And then they need to never be able to hurt anyone ever again.

But it's not until I think of my mom that I feel the rage I see in Olivia.

My mom loved me. Every night she was with me, I went to bed after being tucked in by my mother and knowing, really knowing, I was loved.

I spent years questioning what I did wrong to make her not want me anymore, if she ever wanted me at all, and if any of the love I felt from her was ever real. I tainted every memory of her running her fingers tenderly through my hair before twisting it into a braid. I tainted every good memory of her with doubt, all because of Dominant Point.

I thought maybe the last time she hugged me she was disgusted to be touching me. Maybe I annoyed her too much by crawling into her bed when I had nightmares. Maybe every time our room was pitch black at bed time, and I told her goodnight and I love her, she was really rolling her eyes before saying it back.

They didn't just take her away from me, they took her memory too. All she wanted was to live and get away from me so I would be safe, and they killed her. All because some fucking idiot left to door cracked.

I don't even know what happened to her body. She could've just been dumped in the ocean or thrown away like nothing. Like she's nothing but lifeless flesh.

Not a mother.

Not someone's daughter.

Not someone's friend.

They didn't care about her so she was nothing.

None of it was her fault. She never hated. And they took my mother from me.

I've spent years craving a hug from her, trying to understand what's so awful about me that even my own mother finds me unlovable, because of *them*.

It's such a physical rage, unlike anything I've ever felt before. I can feel it in the veins of my wrist, the urge to just start hitting any of the people responsible. Every muscle in my body aches with anger, craves to hurt them so badly.

Along with it, there's a heavy, deep, sinking emptiness in my chest. It's like my whole body is off balance, empty of everything but anger.

I want my mom back.

And I want to hurt the people who made sure I will never have that.

I grab Olivia's hand and give a single squeeze before letting go to wrap my whole arm around her. We stay like that for a while.

We're here for each other. We understand the love we've lost, we understand what it's like to wonder why a parent wouldn't stay and how could Dominant Point kill our only parent left? Even if we experienced that confusion and death in different ways. And most importantly we understand each other's anger.

She sniffles a few times, tucks a strand of hair behind her ear, then sits up straighter.

"I'm okay. I just hadn't ever told anyone what it was like taking care of my dad or how I went kind of crazy. It made sense to me, but imagining someone else feeding and cuddling a rotting corpse...it's disturbing.

"I've always made myself push those angry thoughts to the back of my head. But saying it out loud doesn't make me feel like a monster like I thought it would, it feels right." She puts on the best smile she can, her face still stained with tears, her cheeks red and splotchy.

I don't believe her at all when she says she's okay. I believe she has hope again. And I believe that *eventually* she'll be okay, but no one is just fine a few weeks after tending to–and cuddling–their dad's dead body.

I don't push her about it though.

I don't tell her that I understand. I don't say I know it's not okay and it doesn't feel like it ever will be. At least not until every last member of Dominant Point has been ripped apart in front of the whole world watching, and maybe not even after that either.

Instead, I let her cover it all back up. I let her pretend everything's okay.

She stands and walks over to her closet, which is much emptier now because of me, and crouches down to grab something. Her shoulders are still shaking as she faces away, but by the time she turns around she's still again. Composed.

"Foragers brought back a bunch of books last week. I've finished most of them, and it's not time to give them back for a few more days." She says as she drops a small pile of books on the bed. "Take your pick."

I eye the spines of each book before deciding to just close my eyes and pick one at random. When I open them again, I'm holding a copy of *A Knight in Shining Leather and Cuffs*.

"Not that one!" Olivia snatches the book out of my hands. "Try this one instead."

She shoves a fantasy novel into my lap titled *The Magic of Hearts*. I look up to see a shy blush growing across Olivia's cheeks.

"Well I didn't write it!" She defends, motioning her hand towards the book she snatched from me.

"No, but you picked it out." I tease.

"Shut up." One of her pillows gently smacks me in the face. She grabs another book from her pile and plops down beside.

I read through the book she chose for me, letting myself be pulled into the world of dragons, witches, mythical creatures, and a prince with wings who's impossible not to love.

No Dominant Point, no sickness, no dead mother, no deadly secrets. Just characters, magic, and love.

I keep reading until the weight of the pages balances evenly between both my hands and my eyes start to close under the weight of my blissfully heavy eyelids.

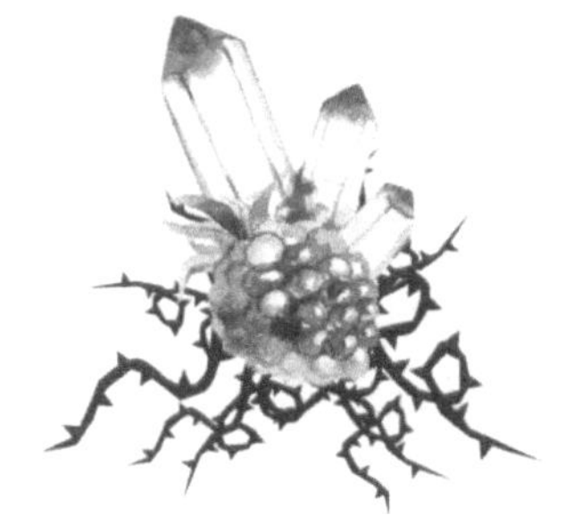

CHAPTER 30

ISABELLE

Liam, Olivia, Vance, and I all sit together while waiting for Ryder to get his breakfast. We had all arrived around the same time, but a little kid cut in front of Ryder and me in line. When we finally got to the front, she decided I could go ahead because she liked my braid. Ryder didn't make the cut.

I watch him now as he picks up different foods for his tray. He seemed uneasy when he first walked in. I tried to ask what was going on, but he said he couldn't talk about it right then.

He looks...like he's maybe okay.

I woke up a while before Olivia this morning, but I stayed still. I couldn't stop imagining her curled up against a dead body with a desperate smile on her face, trying to pretend he was still there, tears running down her cheeks. Just thinking about how her voice cracked, how her face fell when she said she didn't want him to be gone, it was heartbreaking.

I started thinking of things I could tell Kaito. I want us to help people, and not just take in a few lucky ones here and there.

I was okay with knowing that Ryder and I would never be able to help the people who didn't know Dominant Point was doing this to them when we were only going to King Archer's uncle's cabin.

There would've been nothing we could do besides expose ourselves and get killed before we could warn a single person about what was really happening. That wouldn't have helped anyone.

Even though it would have bothered me, knowing people were hurting while we were safe, I would've been able to handle the knowledge that we couldn't help them.

But after everything Kaito has done here for these people, there must be some way to do more. He has true safety here, that's got to count for something. I don't have a plan of what exactly we could do. But I know I'm going to tell him that we need to, and can, do something.

No one should ever have to hold the body of the last person they love for days, because they so badly want to believe that person couldn't have died such an awful, gruesome death right before their eyes.

Olivia seemed like she was in a better mood this morning. But before we fell asleep everything she said to lighten the mood, or even just smile, seemed like she was trying so hard not to cry.

Watching her try so hard to hold it together was worse than watching her cry. I wonder how much it affects her. I understand that losing a parent is hard, but my situation was nothing like hers.

I didn't have to sleep next to my mom's body to convince myself she wasn't gone. I didn't watch her suffer, helpless to ease her pain. And I have no idea what it feels like to love a father instead of a mother.

Does she ever wake up in the morning thinking she's still there next to him? For years after my mom left, I would say good morning to her before I remembered she wasn't there.

Watching the way Olivia and Vance look at each other right now, how they smile every time the other one speaks, it makes me really glad he's here, even if I don't know him very well.

"How are you doing this morning, Belle?" Liam asks.

"Belle?" I repeat. No one's ever called me that. Not even Ryder or my mom

"Just trying something new. You don't like it?"

"Not really, *Iam*." I say, half smiling.

"Well, that's just a stupid nickname–"

Ryder squeezes in across from me with his tray in hand. The first thing he does is grab a napkin and take out a pen. He leans over slightly, keeping his movements casual, discreet.

"Are you okay?" I whisper, leaning forward just enough that only he can hear.

He stays silent and slides the napkin over to me, the pen resting on top.

Are you sure we can really trust Kaito?

I jerk my head up.

"Ye–" I cut my self off when Ryder silently motions towards the napkin.

Yes, I'm sure. What's going on?

I slide it back to him.

Next to Ryder, Olivia and Lance are still completely wrapped up in each other and beside me, Liam has started talking to a four or five year old little boy who's watching him like he just invented cake.

Ryder writes back.

He was acting strange last night. I just want to be sure that you truly believe we can trust him.

Kaito raised me. He helped my mom out of his own kindness. He's given us a safe place to stay. We can trust him. I start to write that on the last bit of space left on the napkin but hesitate.

Kaito *is* a royal who was training to go to Dominant Point. And all those good deeds...they don't really make sense. He didn't get anything out of helping my mom or saving any of us.

But him being evil wouldn't make sense either. There's no good reason for him to have done all this, save all these people, then say 'No, I'm actually evil and I'm going to eat you or something'.

Yes.

That's all I write.

I pass the napkin back and try to give him a look that says I'm absolutely sure I trust Kaito. And if all he wants to talk about is if *I* trust him, then we're done talking.

Still, he flips to the back side and writes something else on the napkin then passes it back to me.

Okay, I trust you, and you trust him.

I pass the note back to him and smile.

I *do* trust Kaito.

I believe that no matter what he does, even if it ends up inconveniencing Ryder and me, he'll do so with good intentions. No matter what Ryder ends up telling me Kaito did to make him doubt him, I'm sure there will be a fine explanation.

Ryder twists the napkin at an odd angle, probably looking for a space that isn't already covered in ink, and squeezes in another message.

'While everyone else is finishing breakfast, would you like to come with me back to the surface? We can have our own spot just for us, like we used to.'

I look up at him, my lip between my teeth, then grab the pen sitting atop the napkin. I flick it back and forth between my fingers, thinking of a cute way to say yes, before just settling on a simple yes and a smiley face. Before my pen even touches the napkin, a voice I thought I'd never hear again rips the air from my lungs.

"Ryder?"

No.

It *can't* be.

I look over Ryder's head with wide eyes and my heart sinks to my stomach.

There she is.

Blonde hair, button nose, beautiful freckled face, and green eyes.

The long dead Princess Anastasia of Sirius.

Ryder's brows pinch together as his mouth falls open, clearly recognizing the voice behind him, before he quickly turns around and shoots out of his seat. The moment her eyes land on him, she breaks into the brightest ear to ear smile and lets out a choked sob.

Olivia watches the scene with furrowed brows, then shifts to give me a sympathetic look. Next to me, Liam gapes at the supposedly dead girl.

Princess Anastasia takes wide, fast steps towards Ryder. He finally snaps out of his frozen state.

"How-"

She cuts him off, grabbing his face with both hands, and kissing him like he's always been hers.

CHAPTER 31

ISABELLE

"When did you get here? Why are you here? Are you okay?"

She runs her hands up and down his shoulders, looking over him, taking him all in. She seems oblivious to him backing away from her every touch.

The two of them look just as right together as they did a few years ago. Two of a kind.

When they first got together, Ryder told me how good it felt to talk to someone who knew what all the pressure and expectations felt like. I don't think he realized how much it hurt when he said that. *I* had always been the one who understood him no matter what. Then suddenly, I wasn't.

I wonder how relieved he is to have her back. To be able to go through all this with someone who actually *understands* him. Instead of someone whose biggest responsibility was plants and bringing people their plate.

I didn't like her much back then. I didn't like the way she looked at me, or the way she snapped her fingers at me like I was a dog whenever she needed something. But I could always admit to myself that she and Ryder fit together perfectly. They look like they still do. Same confident posture. Same elegant mannerisms. Same striking good looks.

"We've been here a few days now." Liam interrupts Anastasia fawning over his brother. Her brows knit together, her mouth slightly agape.

"Everyone was talking about them the moment they got here," Olivia points out. "You would've known they were here."

Realization dawns over Anastasia's face. She quickly shakes her head.

"The foragers brought in some new books last week and there were a lot of really good options. I've been in my room all day, every day, since then, I've barely talked to anyone."

She laughs and turns back to Ryder. Her face lights up at the sight of him. "There are a few I think you will really like. God, I'm so happy to see you."

She leans in for another kiss but Ryder quickly pulls back, as if her lips may have acid on them. She deflates a little, her head tilting in confusion.

"Isabelle?" Ryder asks. His voice is gentle but laced with urgency. Anastasia slowly turns her head towards me, her eyes clinging Ryder until the last second. Her rapid thoughts race just behind her eyes. Anastasia's gaze settles on me, direct and hot, like I might burst into flames at any second.

"Will you please come with me?" Ryder nods towards the hall. I quickly drop the fork that's been frozen in my grasp since I first saw that long gone blonde hair.

I nod, and before I can make it to my feet, Olivia grabs me by my arm and leans in to whisper in my ear, "I'm so sorry. I thought you guys all knew you were here. I figured maybe there was just some kind of royal drama between you all, and that's why I hadn't seen you guys in the same room since you arrived." She loosens her grip on my arm, sympathy written across her face.

"It's okay."

Anastasia looks back and forth between Ryder, Liam, me, Olivia, and even Vance. When I meet Ryder at the end of the table his hand rests on the small of my back to guide us out. I look over my shoulder and see the moment something clicks behind her eyes.

She looks back and forth between us, then at the others, waiting for someone to make sense of what's happening.

She watches me with a disgusted, hateful look. Like I'm something filthy she accidently brushed against. It's enough to bring up every insecurity I've ever had while watching Ryder be with people like him. Like I'll always just be beneath them in a way that's so obvious to anyone watching. I'm an outsider playing dress up as someone equal enough to be his friend.

Ryder interlocks his fingers with mine as I look ahead of us and away from her. I don't want to see whatever look she would be giving me now.

Once we've turned the hall, he drops my hand and leans against the wall, squeezing his eyes shut for a moment and running his hands down his face. He's silent for a while. A million thoughts flash through his expression while I try my hardest to read all of them.

"I'm sorry," he whispers. Before I can take in his tone or expression I finish that sentence on my own.

I'm sorry, but I still love her. I'm sorry, but now that she's back, I know I never want to leave her side again. I'm sorry but it'll always be her.

He runs his hand gently up my forearm.

"I didn't kiss her back. I stood there because I was in shock, but I didn't kiss her back." I couldn't tell if he had.

His back had been tense and his hands were frozen at his sides but the moment I saw her face, all I could see was every time I saw them kiss when they were together. How she looked at him with just as much love in her eyes then as she has for him now. Without being able to see his face myself, my memory filled in the blank for me.

Even though remembering what it was like to watch them kiss each other a few years ago isn't a nice memory right now, I know he never reacted like that. Although, she hadn't just come back from the dead any of those times.

"I know," I say, and he visibly relaxes. A small smile touches my lips as he gives me a quick kiss on the cheek, then beelines down the hall with our hands still together.

I assume he's probably taking us to the surface, but I don't ask. I glance at Ryder and see the unspoken question clearly written across his face, the same one I've been asking myself.

How the hell is she here?

When we were told about what happened to the Sirius family, I felt awful about what happened to her and how afraid she must've been when it happened. No one deserves to die that way.

But a small part of me—that I quickly pushed aside—was glad she wouldn't be coming back. It wasn't about her being with Ryder. I didn't understand that I liked him as more than a friend back then, and even if I had, that would never be enough for me to be glad she was dead. It was about *her.*

She wasn't just a royal. She was a royal who knew every privilege in the world belonged to her.

I look back up at Ryder and wonder how much he must've suffered when we thought she died. He seemed hurt, but not devastated.

I assumed he just didn't want to talk about it, which hurts when even your best friend can't talk to you about something. But now, I think he might have just felt exactly how he seemed. It's obvious he isn't exactly ecstatic to have her back.

When she would stay in the palace she would look at me like I was nothing more than someone meant to serve them, and I was.

Every time Ryder spoke to me as a friend instead of ignoring my presence, she would give me this look like I should be grateful to even be in the same room as them.

Ryder lets go of my hand to pound on Kaito's door. I hadn't even realized he was taking us here.

Kaito swings the door open with a tense expression from the aggressive knocks. His face softens once his gaze lands on Ryder.

"What the hell is she doing here?" Ryder asks.

Kaito's gaze drops to me. "It looks like you brought her here?"

"Anastasia," Ryder clarifies, his voice cold as ice. I hate the sound of her name on his lips. Kaito's face shifts to understanding, confusion again, then annoyance.

"Oh, same thing as absolutely every other person here. She's here because this is what's safest for her. I'm sure you can piece two and two together given your high royal education, albeit with a few plot holes, but it's not my place to tell you her business or why she ended up here." Kaito stands firm at the door, not welcoming us in.

"Why wouldn't you tell us she was here? You had to have known we knew each other." Ryder presses.

I stand off to the side, watching the exchange like a fly on the wall.

I haven't missed this feeling. But, it does give me some privacy, even out in the open to feel invisible.

"I didn't realize you expected me to be your personal matchmaker for meeting everyone else living in The Haven. I have a long list of things to attend to every day and nowhere on that list do I concern myself with a teenager's social life." Kaito replies coolly.

"If this revelation of me having my own duties that don't revolve entirely around you or Anastasia has upset you, I apologize. But there are bigger things to worry about. Is there anything else you need?"

For the very first time in our lives I watch Ryder bite his tongue for someone other than his father. He doesn't say anything as he turns away.

Kaito gives me a slight nod before shutting his office door.

We're silent as Ryder leads us to the ladder up to the surface. The tension rolls off his shoulders in waves. It's not until we're outside, with a gentle breeze in the air, long grass beneath our feet, and the smell of ocean salt flooding our noses, that the thoughts racing through my mind finally fade into the background.

"Are you okay?" I ask as I sit. He follows me and I rest my head on his shoulder.

"Yes. Just...surprised, is all." His body feels rigid and tense against mine.

"It's okay if you're not...okay. You don't have to pretend to feel nothing for my sake. I know this must be a lot." I think if he starts talking about how much he loves her, I'll puke. I feel his shoulders start to relax beneath my head.

"I liked her. Well, I'm not sure it was *her* that I liked exactly, but the new things I got to experience with her."

Please, please, please don't go into detail about the 'new things'.

"She was an important step in my life. When I found out she was dead, I was upset that I lost someone who knew so much about me and who had been a part of my life. But I didn't feel like I lost someone I loved or couldn't live without. Seeing her after years of believing she was dead...it just felt like rereading a book I had put away a long time ago, at least in terms of how I felt about her."

A strong, selfish, relief floods through me. From the moment I saw her, I thought I might be the worst person in the world.

Instead of being happy she was okay, I just wanted her to be gone again. That awful, bitter feeling twisted my gut like it was turning me green from the inside out.

I hate it. I don't ever want to be the kind of person who's this selfish. I look over my shoulder at the large field stretching out into trees, knowing that on the other side of that forest, people are suffering unimaginably. And I'm here, upset over an ex-girlfriend.

It's stupid and selfish and every tear that welled in my eyes when I saw her was entirely self centered. People on the other side of those trees shed their tears over their children's corpses.

I knew it the moment the first ping of pain hit my chest. It didn't make it stop hurting, if anything it hurt more.

It feels a little ridiculous. When we were up here last time, I guess it seemed so official something had changed when we kissed. But really we didn't talk about it. There's a chance that it could've just been a kiss and nothing more. No discovered feelings. No new kind of relationship between us.

But when I think about the look in his eyes before it happened, the way he watched me, the tender yet needy way he kissed me, it had to mean more.

It had to.

I've stood in the same old, uncomfortable, stiff, scratchy, jumpsuit while people my age walked around in the most beautiful dresses I've ever seen. They'd complain about things I would've loved to have, and still, I never felt hateful or envious. I felt like my outfit was itchy, they looked beautiful in that dress, or that my feet hurt.

They had what they had because of how they were born. I had what I had because of how I was born. It's not fair but it's not their fault.

There's only one difference between then and what I felt when I saw Anastasia and her stupid, perfect blond hair, or heard her annoyingly beautiful Siriusian accent.

Whenever I've had a nightmare, it's been his bed that I crawled into. When we were little and he was afraid of his dad being in a bad mood, it was me he would grab to hide in the closet with. He was the one who made me feel like it didn't matter if I had my servant's uniform on or the most expensive, beautifully tailored dress in the kingdom. I was more than beautiful every time he looked at me. That feeling of real recognition only really mattered to me when it was from him.

Our kiss meant something more, I know it did. I also know that no matter how much better it makes everything feel to have this new thing with Ryder, or how much it may have hurt to be afraid I was losing it, it's not what's most important.

"Why were you asking me if we could trust Kaito?"

Ryder shuts his eyes and tilts his head back, the wind gently flowing through his dark brown hair.

"I was looking for him and when I found him, he just disappeared. There wasn't anywhere else he could've walked away to that quickly. I know it doesn't sound like much, but he was acting suspicious. It just felt wrong, like he was hiding something."

I try to think of some of the worst case scenarios for all the things he could be hiding. Unless he has every Dominant Point representative living in a secret basement ready to kill us all, I don't think whatever it is could be *that* bad. We don't know *everything* about him, and he's bound to have some secrets, but we do know he's given so many people a safe place when they needed it.

"It's probably nothing to worry about. He's a good person. At the end of the day, I'm sure he has good intentions, no matter what secrets he may have." I say.

"Good intentions don't necessarily mean good actions, and we don't know if his 'good intentions' would be directed at us or himself," he says.

He *is* very focused on protecting his people, and we don't know if he entirely includes us in that group. No matter why everyone else is here, Liam, Ryder, and I are important to Dominant Point. Maybe Kaito could sell us out to them for something that would help the rest of his people. Or maybe not.

"Well, if he does kill us, you can say you told me so." I say.

"Then I guess it'll be worth it." He smiles.

He's beautiful right now. He's more relaxed than he ever seems when we're inside The Haven. His hair blows smoothly in the wind, the light shines down on his skin, and most importantly his smile, while small, is genuine.

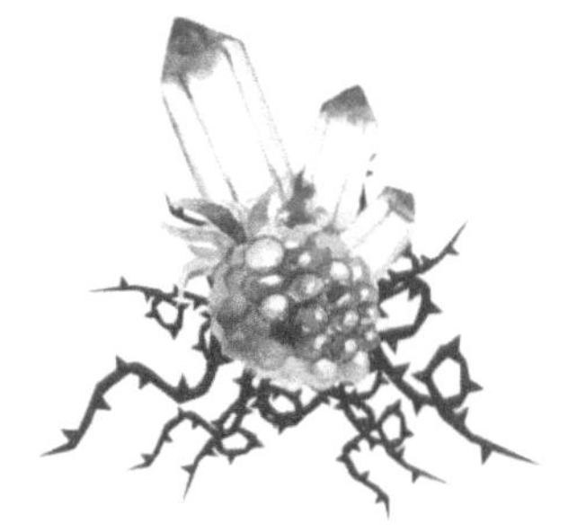

CHAPTER 32

RYDER

Maybe I should feel bad for Anastasia. With the way her face lit up the moment she saw me, it's obvious she thought we were something more than we were. We said we loved each other, but looking back now, it was puppy love.

We shared new experiences with each other. We were more intimate than we had ever been with anyone else and it's easy to confuse that with love. But that's still not what it was.

In truth, despite knowing she must've been through something horrible, and knowing with as much certainty as I can—which isn't much considering the two supposedly dead people here—that she has lost her family, I was only annoyed that she would kiss me in front of Isabelle like we were star crossed lovers finally reunited.

The uncertainty and blatant hurt on Isabelle's face when I turned around from Anastasia's unwelcomed affection hit me a thousand times harder than whatever Anasatsia's sob story is. Seeing Isabelle glance between us and look down at her plate like she was losing something made my chest ache.

She's been quiet ever since I explained how I felt about Anastasia. Her head resting on my shoulder feels so different yet just as right as every other time we've sat like this.

The wind brushing the stray hair of her halo braid, letting it tickle my neck, and the faint sound of her breathing feels like something truly solid to hold onto amidst all the confusion and chaos.

I have no idea how Anastasia got out of that fire. I don't know what the last few years have been like for her, and right now, I don't really care. I'm in no rush to go back inside. Back to all the drama, risen dead people, and shattered perceptions.

I know, given how close we once were, I should care more. The fact that I don't makes me horrible, mainly because I know my father would be proud. But then again, he would also beat me senseless if he knew how much I care for Isabelle, so maybe it levels out.

I rise to my feet and hold out a hand for Isabelle.

"Come on,"

She hesitantly reaches for my hand as she tilts her head. "You're ready to go back in already?" I lift her to her feet.

"God no. I want to go down there." I nod towards the water. She visibly relaxes, and a small smile tugs at my lips.

Maybe I never felt incredibly close to Anastasia, because deep down, I knew Isabelle was the only one I could ever feel this connected to.

I hold her hand a little tighter as we make our way down the steep, rocky hill towards the beach. We slide every few feet, loose dirt and gravel shifting beneath us, until we finally reach the flat, sandy beach.

Isabelle drops my hand the moment we're down and takes off towards the water. She bunches up the bottom of her dress in her hands and dips her toes in until she's knee deep, being pushed back by the waves every few seconds.

She looks over her shoulder at me with a shy smile. I start to grab the hem of my shirt to pull it off but pause when I see her slide her dress up her body and over her head. We've gone swimming in our underwear at least a million times, but watching her now feels different.

Now, seeing her nearly naked isn't expected to be simply platonic. I let my eyes sweep over her and pause longer than I had ever let myself before.

She laughs and turns her face away. When she looks back at me she has a beautiful, shy, ear to ear smile and a blush growing on her cheeks.

"Come on." She reaches her hands out for me, and once I'm close enough she goes deep enough into the water that I'm sure her feet aren't touching.

"I missed playing in the river with you so much," she says, almost sadly, despite her smile. I don't think it's just the river she's talking about, but everything from before she read her mom's journal, before the fear and uncertainty and misplaced guilt.

I do too.

I swim out to her, my feet only inches above the sand, and relax. Now that we've both silently agreed we don't want to go back in any time soon, she's perked up a little bit.

I understood a long time ago why my father was so adamant that I couldn't care for anyone besides him and my mother, not even my brother. He said that in my position, caring was dangerous. I didn't get it until Isabelle and

I were seven and nine. We were chasing each other outside and we tripped over the other one's feet. We scraped up our knees and elbows, and as soon as I saw her eyes start to tear up I couldn't care less about my own injury. I just wanted her to feel better.

Every day that I've loved her, I've cared more about her than myself. After kissing her and knowing I want to be able to kiss her every day for the rest of my life, that feeling has only grown stronger.

And it hurts, like having my heart outside my own body.

I will never be going to Dominant Point. I won't ever hold the kind of power I once thought I would, the kind that made my father so afraid of me caring for someone this much. Still, the twist in my gut at the thought of not always being able to make her feel better tells me it's still just as dangerous as he always warned.

"I love you." The words leave my mouth with little thought and no hesitation. I don't even entirely realize I've said them until I feel the last word slip out.

"I love you too." She smiles. Not seeming taken aback or surprised in the slightest. We've said this to each other a thousand times before, but this time the exact same words mean something completely different.

"No." I shake my head, chewing on the inside of my cheek while I think of the right words, suddenly much more nervous than when I said it a second ago. This time feels so much more real.

"I love you the way Anakin loves Evelyn."

She read that book when she was thirteen, and she's read it a hundred times since. She used to go on about it for hours, telling me about what was happening like she was talking about real people.

Her eyes widen, she tucks her lip under her teeth, holding back a smile that stretches ear to ear and lights up her face as she says, "I love you like Evelyn loves Anakin."

She paddles her arms to get a bit closer to me and wraps her arms around my neck, using me to float. I watch as the lonely look from earlier fades from her expression, replaced by a confidence I've rarely seen in her.

I love it.

I'll compare every one of her favorite romances to how I feel about her, every day, just to see this look of absolute confidence on her again and again.

I love her. I admire her.

Everything about her is so uniquely beautiful; how kindly she interacts with the other servant's children, her curiosity, her strange passion for the lives of people who only exist in just ink on paper, her anger when we were kids and she first found out about my father hurting me.

It's her love and her rage, every aspect of her. Every slight shift in her expression showing just who she is.

She's love.

She doesn't just bring it out of people, she radiates it.

CHAPTER 33

ISABELLE

There's an extra bounce in my steps as Ryder and I head down the twisting halls towards the common room, expecting to find Liam in there.

He's been spending most days there lately. It's filled with games, puzzles, books, and most importantly, lots of girls laughing at his jokes like they've never met a man before. Or maybe it's because if things had gone differently he would've been their king.

Ryder and I stayed on the surface all day, swimming in the ocean and lying on the sand. Dinner is pretty soon, and while I wouldn't trade that time we spent out there for anything, I do worry someone will notice we were missing all day and Kaito will find out we've been going to the surface.

I'm not sure what would happen if he does, but I know it wouldn't be good. Whether it's him saying he's disappointed or handing out an actual punishment, both make me just as nervous.

Still, I wasn't in any rush to get back inside to avoid being caught. We swam together, played, and splashed. It was the best day I've had in a while. I wasn't thinking about the murders in Dominant Point, the sickness ripping through people, or Anastasia. Selfishly, I just enjoyed the moment.

We kissed while I wrapped my legs around him in the water. We laid in the sand, grains sticking to our skin, as he ran his fingers over my wet hair.

It makes me want to ask Olivia an extra journal she may be hiding anywhere just to write down this one memory while it's fresh and keep it forever. I think back to what she said when she was talking about Vance. She would think I'm so stupid if she knew I told him I loved him after one kiss.

But I do love him.

I've known him my whole life, and I've always known, without a shadow of a doubt, he's my person. I just never acknowledged the possibility it might not be a platonic love.

I think deep down I knew that when he left one day to go to Dominant Point, it would hurt so much more if it was after I had decided I wanted to really be with him for the rest of my life. Losing someone who makes every love interest I've read about in romances seem like nothing in comparison, hurts a lot more than losing my best friend who was always going to marry someone like Anastasia and have little royal babies that I would work for when I got old.

We're a long way from what we were supposed to be doing right now. He would probably be getting ready to train in the outer layers of Dominant Point, and I would be bracing myself to lose him, as a friend.

As soon as we round the corner to the common room, we see Liam leaning against the pool table, arms crossed and a smirk on his face as he talks to a few girls. I recognize a few of them. The redhead and the dirty blonde both asked me if he was single the other day. They seemed nice, so I told them to go for it.

Once he sees us, he apologizes to his fan club, flashes his signature flirty smile, and walks over to meet us at the closest table. Ryder and I take the two seats next to each other. Liam drops into the one across from us, raising an eyebrow.

"Why do I feel like you're not planning an epic proposal for your long lost, previously thought to be charred, love? Also, while you were out breaking dead girls' hearts, I was confirming our safety with smooth, charming intel gathering. I still don't think there are any plans to eat our toes or sacrifice us to an evil spirit, but it does seem like *something* is going on, I'm just not sure if it's a bad thing."

"First of all," Ryder says, clearly annoyed, "we were together three years ago, and we were only kids. Time didn't pause and we weren't in love. Secondly, what's going on?"

"Don't worry about it. I'll let you know if I think we're going to die," Liam shrugs, waving his hand in the air. "And it doesn't seem like she got the memo." Liam laughs, bringing us back to the part he clearly finds most interesting.

"I mean, did you see the way she looked at you? Five more seconds and blue birds would have flown in chirping love songs."

Remembering the way she looked at him doesn't make me feel much more than embarrassment for her now.

The realization is an imminent relief. Maybe now I can look at her being here with empathy for whatever happened to her, instead of the disgusting, hateful feeling I felt this morning.

I wanted to puke at the idea I could be so cruel as to feel that way when she didn't really do anything wrong. All she did was survive.

"Anyhoo," Liam mumbles, "what the hell happened to her?"

"Obviously, she survived the fire and The Haven took her in," Ryder deadpans, staring at Liam with the kind of bored look reserved for truly stupid questions.

"No shit, I mean in more detail. Like an actual explanation. One that's more interesting than what you just said." Liam rolls his eyes.

"I sincerely apologize if the story of my whole family burning to death in my childhood home isn't entertaining enough." The calm words slip out of her mouth beautifully with her smooth Siriusian accent.

Liam's face immediately reddens, and a small smile tugs at Ryder's lips watching his brother falter. "Uh, if it helps, I actually wasn't sure if they were really dead. Since, you know, you and Kaito were both supposed to be gone."

Anastasia starts to say something but stops when Kaito walks into the room.

He looks *angry*.

I've only talked to him a few times since I've been here, and he doesn't seem very easy to anger. He was annoyed this morning, but this is far from annoyed.

His eyes sweep across the room before locking onto us. My stomach twists under the heat of his gaze.

"Ryder. May I speak with you, please?" he bites out.

Ryder appears unfazed by Kaito's harsh tone. He stands then leans into my ear, "I'll be back shortly," he whispers, before following Kaito out.

"Weird," Liam mutters as he watches them walk away.

Anastasia takes Ryder's empty seat and stares me down through her crystal green eyes. "Olivia tells me you and Ryder are together. She was actually very quick to tell me once you two left breakfast so abruptly. Is it true?"

Out of the corner of my eye, I see Liam's neck nearly snap as he whips his head towards me and drops his jaw so low I would've believed he dislocated it.

I muster up all the confidence I felt back on the beach with Ryder and straighten my back, "Yes, we are."

Anger flashes through her eyes, but it's quickly masked by sympathy. "You poor thing. You must've hated seeing him kiss me earlier. Seeing him back with his own people must have stung, given what you are."

I deflate a little bit but keep my back straight and my head high. "Not when I watched him push you off."

A quick, small laugh bursts out of Liam, but cuts off the moment we turn to look at him. "What?" Liam asks.

Anastasia ignores him and turns back to me.

"You don't get to speak to me that way. Since I first started studying abroad at the Adhara palace, when we were kids, it has been your job to serve me. You hang my coat. You serve my food. You serve me and everyone else who is above you."

"Don't be a bitch. You-" Liam starts but Anastasia cuts him off, never taking her eyes off me.

"I know you probably wished I was dead the moment you saw me, but I haven't done anything wrong. I never even got an actual break up.

"My entire family, but one brother and my mother, all burned to *death* with my childhood home because of some Dominant Point secret and I was meant to die with them. Instead, I had snuck out to look at the flowers before the fire was set. After everything I had was gone, I spent *days* sleeping in tree branches, dirty, alone, afraid, and wanting my family back, until The Haven found me and took me in.

"I've spent the last *three years* here thinking that I would never see the boy I loved ever again. I thought, if only he were here, we would still be together and I would still have at least one really good thing left. And then he did show up, only for me to see that he couldn't have forgotten me fast enough, and had already stooped low enough to think he wants some servant!

"I didn't even get a break up. So me kissing him when I thought the love of my life had found his way back to me wasn't some evil thing. However mean you think it was for me to kiss him, the way you looked at me was just plain cruel." She's practically seething.

I've never seen the ever regal princess of Sirius show more disdain than a scowl or hateful smirk. My heart cracks at the thought of what she's been through, and what she must've felt having Ryder reject her.

"I'm sorry-"

"Don't be. If I were you, I wouldn't want me around either. I have received the highest education in the world since the moment I was born. I speak all six languages fluently and have been regarded as the most beautiful girl in the world since I was twelve.

"You may not still work as a servant, but who we are hasn't changed. You're the uneducated girl who never learned to wear her hair more than one way, never wore anything but a scratchy, ugly, unflattering uniform, and never made a difference that any other mindless drone couldn't make. You're the same now.

I'm actually *useful* here. All you do is eat our food and take up space that could be for people who actually have a functioning brain and more than some stupid servant's education. Your entire purpose in life was to serve people like me and Ryder. Nothing more. The day that you would've died, the only sorrow would've been the annoyance of whoever has to throw your rotting body out and replace your servants quarters with someone equally as unimportant." She delivers every word like the clean cut of a blade, looking at me with complete sincerity.

I completely deflate. The last part of what she said wasn't even said with anger or cruelty like before, just brutal honesty. Every ounce of confidence I had been able to pull together is gone, and the worst part is how easy that was.

If someone had just tried to hurt her like that, she wouldn't have cared. She would've known that she's worth being confident.

Every thing she just said hit a tender spot that I hate she can see, and it *hurts,* but not as much as knowing that it shouldn't be that easy.

I should be able to be confident with or without Ryder's reassurance, and hold onto it even when someone clearly aims to hurt me. Not being able to bring myself to feel that way evokes so much more self doubt than what she could ever say to me.

A few tears start to burn the back of my eyes, making me feel even worse. I look through the corner of my blurry eyes and see Liam *fuming*.

"Fuck. Off. Accept the fact that you may be a pretty, blonde, princess while she's 'just a servant' and she's still more likable than you, a better person than you, and most of all, someone Ryder could actually give a shit about. He doesn't care about you so *get over it*."

She stares at him, slack jawed. She opens and closes her mouth a few times, but never settles on the right thing to say. And I may be crazy, but I think she looks a little teary eyed.

Maybe she's not as independently confident as I thought. Maybe she just has better posture than me and a resting superiority complex on her face.

She looks down, regains her composer, and walks away without a single word, elegance in every step. I blink away the last of the tears in my eyes, honestly and shamefully a little amused by her reaction, and turn back to Liam.

"Are you and Ryder really together?" He asks, raising an eyebrow.

"Since yesterday, or this morning," I say. Officially this morning, but yesterday too.

"Finally. You guys have been staring at each other like love struck puppies for years. It's sickening. Also, entirely unfair. You've been looking at each other like you're made of sugar for years and only *just now* decided you're not only friends. *I* understand romance and how to take a hint, but where's *my* girl to make people nauseous with how we look at each other?"

I burst out a choked laugh. I've never appreciated his humor more than right now, after I almost cried in front of everyone here.

"It looked like you had quite a lot of volunteers earlier," I point out.

He rolls his eyes, "They just want my pretty face and toned arms. Seriously though, I'm happy for you two. It's about time. And I'm glad he has you with everything that's going on."

He would've had me if we were still just friends, but I don't point that out.

"He seems like he's doing better with this place. He knows we're safe here now." I say.

I don't think he'll ever believe he's absolutely safe anywhere. He's been raised to believe someone always wants him dead. But I think he knows this place is as safe as it can be. Most importantly, we can trust the people here.

"I don't think he would be shocked if someone here tried to kill him, but sure. I'm talking about our mom. He told me Kaito said contacting her was a no go. You know how much she's always meant to him. Not being able to tell her he's okay must be killing him."

Honestly, with everything else that's happened since then, I haven't thought to check on him again. He seemed so heart broken when Kaito said we couldn't contact her.

"What about you? You love her too," I say.

"Yeah but it's different for me. He was so close to our mom because of how awful our dad was to him. He always got worse from him than I did. Don't get me wrong, I have my fair share of scars from our father, literally, but Ryder was the one going to Dominant Point, the one who would have the most power. So our father was always harder on him. I mean, you *know* what our dad would do to him. You've seen it. After that, our mother was always there for him.

"They're closer than me and her are, and given the reason why I don't really mind. But it must suck for him to not be able to help her when she's always been there for him."

I remember when I was little and Ryder's dad first started hitting him. I would search all over the palace for him.

Once I found him, he told me he was hiding from his dad with his mom.

Ryder and Liam's dad never hit their mom, though. He's never even raised his voice at her. He's an awful father and if he does know about what Dominant Point's doing, I don't think he would be opposed to it, but he's a really good husband.

He would die for his wife, and he loves her exactly as she is. But in his eyes his sons are just future leaders who need to be taught and punished to become the best.

So obviously, the one who will have a seat in deciding what happens to people all across the world would need a firmer, tougher hand to *teach* him.

"Does he-" I cut myself off, distracted by a boy and girl talking a few feet away from us.

"King Archer's dead?" the girl asks the boy. "What happened?"

"Not sure, Kaito just wrote that he's dead. He was poisoned so it was probably Dominant Point." The boy shrugs.

"Where did you hear that?" I ask, shooting out of my seat. As soon as the boy turns his head my way, he looks from me to someone behind me.

"Isabelle. Liam. Would you come with us?" It's Kaito.

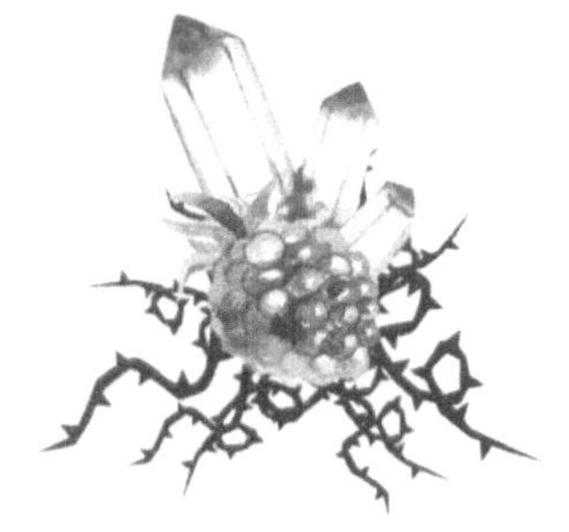

CHAPTER 34

ISABELLE

"I s King Archer dead?" I blurt as soon as Liam and I catch up to Kaito. He's already making his way down the hall.

He looks down for a moment, I'm guessing he and Archer were close.

"Yes, I found out yesterday that Archer was found dead in the morning." He shakes his head, as if he's shaking off whatever he feels about King Archer's death, then continues walking down the hall.

Dominant Point must've found out he helped us and assumed that meant he knew about their responsibility for the sickness. Maybe they didn't care about if he knew, maybe helping us was enough of a reason to kill him.

My chest feels heavy, like my heart's being pulled down. It's not grief, I hardly knew him. It's guilt.

Princess Marcella, Prince Dustin, and Queen Victoria must be devastated. He seemed like an amazing father and husband. I can picture Victoria holding her children as the three of them sob, whatever it feels like to be loved by a father being stripped away from Marcella and Dustin. All the pressure, all the loss they must be feeling, would they hate me if they knew why he died?

I was a part of someone losing their family too soon, part of an innocent man dying. I try to tell myself all the things I know Ryder would say if I voiced any of this: *you're not responsible for someone else's actions. He chose to help us, and he knew that would have consequences.*

It's not my fault. I did not kill him. But I was still a part of it, a reason that he's dead.

That doesn't make it my fault. It's not my fault. I didn't kill him.

He was a good man, and it's awful that he's dead. He didn't deserve that. I don't need to blame myself. I shouldn't blame myself.

I remember that Kaito seemed a little surprised by my question. He didn't come get us, or pull Ryder aside, to talk about what happened to Archer. I still don't know where he's taking us.

"What did Kaito want to talk to you about?" I lean into Ryder's ear as Kaito leads us through the twisting halls.

"He knows we've been going to the surface, and there's something else that I think would be best to let him explain." he whispers back.

"If he knows we've both been going up there, why did he only talk to you?" I ask.

A small smirk lifts his lips, "He thought I would be more difficult to deal with, so he wanted a moment alone with me."

I guess that explains how angry he seemed when he came to get Ryder.

Kaito suddenly stops and turns to face us, pinning his gaze on me.

"You two are not ever, *ever*, permitted to go to the surface without my knowledge. Do you have any idea how much danger you put us in? What do you think would've happened if someone had seen the missing prince in the middle of nowhere, and then mysteriously disappear beneath the ground? I've kept this place and everyone in it safe for *years*, and I won't allow you two to ruin that safety!" He finishes, his chest huffing in anger. I flinch at the boom in his voice.

I don't think he would ever physically hurt us, but it's unnerving to see someone as welcoming as him be so furious.

He drags a frustrated hand down his face, visibly trying to calm himself. "I understand it wasn't your intention to put us at risk, and I trust that in the future you'll be more careful with your actions. Nonetheless, you will both be covering janitorial duties for the next week. That includes bathrooms,post meal clean up, and anywhere else I see fit."

For me, that's nothing. The only real punishment here is Kaito's anger. But for Ryder? Ex-prince and future Adhara representative? He's going to feel like he's being tortured. Kaito turns back around and continues walking down the hall.

"Is there a reason you're ominously walking us silently down a hallway, without telling us why, or is this just for dramatic effect?" Liam asks.

"I told Ryder the other day that I had a job for the two of you. Anastasia has been a large part of this as well, given her political training and education.

"This place we call The Haven was built centuries ago by the civilians. Before the creation of Dominant Point each country was individually ruled, as you know. Eventually, people began to riot, furious that their lives were dictated by someone simply because of their blood. The queen of Adhara at that time was a blood thirsty psychopath. She killed anyone who stood in her way, tortured her own people, even her family, just for the pleasure of it. She did anything to tighten her grip on power.

"They built this place in preparation for a war against royalty but before it could ever be used, the royals came up with a compromise. Only those with royal blood would rule, but only the most fit among them would hold the most power. Those chosen few would not only look out for their own kingdom, but for the entire world. It was meant to symbolize world peace between the kingdoms. To prove that no one truly awful could be in power again. Should anyone become oppressive, they would promptly be put down, like the queen of Adhara."

"I've never heard of some deranged, bloody-thirsty Queen of Adhara that set Dominant Point into motion. I know the names of every ruler Adhara's ever had, and none of them were as you described." Ryder says.

I haven't heard of her either, but that doesn't mean much. I was only taught the basics of history, each kingdom used to be individual and now we're united. The end.

"Me neither, and I remember some things from history lessons. I would've remembered someone like that. That's not what we were taught." Liam adds.

"That's not what they wanted you to learn. There are plenty of things that have happened throughout history that we don't know about. Some are simply forgotten over time, others are erased. A few centuries ago, Dominant Point decided her legacy was a stain on humanity. She was a murderer who did everything to gain more power. People like that don't deserve to be remembered. They decided it would be a good final 'screw you' for her to be forgotten. So they removed her from the history books, and a few generations later, no one remembered her at all. I didn't find out about her until after I came here. I found very, very old files about her.

"She killed her infant sister and murdered the King of Polaris's son in front of him. She was a monster in every sense of the word and deserves to be forgotten. Erasing her is one of the few good things Dominant Point has done." Kaito finishes with a disgusted look on his face, no doubt from the things he must've read about her. Ryder and Liam don't say anything. Neither of them looks particularly shocked that Dominant Point erased an entire part of history.

"Back to what I was saying, obviously, we've made some technological improvements since finding sanctuary here. But we've also held onto what we discovered here."

He lifts a panel in the wall and types a code into the keypad hidden behind it. A door, perfectly blended into the wall, slides open in front of us.

"*Holy shit,*" Liam whispers.

The 'room' beyond the door is actually about three levels high with an open central space surrounded by railings.

Each level holds large amounts of armor, both modern and ancient. There's weapons like bows, swords, and newer ones like guns, which until now I'd only seen on the men who nearly found us in the woods.

We all know the royals, specifically Dominant Point, have guns. We all know they can be used for mass destruction and what they look like, but most people have never actually seen one.

I glance to my side and see Ryder give me a small smile. He doesn't seem the least bit surprised, unlike Liam and me. I'm guessing this was part of his talk with Kaito.

Kaito steps in front of us and gestures to the entire multilevel room.

"The reason The Haven was built wasn't to provide sanctuary for those who need it. From day one, it's been about taking down those who have abused their power and hurt the people they swore to protect.

"This place was built to be used for a war, and now, eight-hundred years later, it will be."